The door was never meant to be found.

Cabin Zero
Beneath The Pines

Pine Hollow Mystery Book 1

Benjamin Alexandar

An Agragape Publication

CABIN ZERO: BENEATH THE PINES

A Pine Hollow Mystery Book 1

Benjamin Alexandar

Published by Agragape Publications

978-1-7367487-7-0 (paperback)

978-1-7367487-8-7 (e-book)

Editorial and Cover Design by:

JohnEdgar.Design

Affordable and Professional Book Cover, Interior, and Marketing Design

https://www.johnedgar.design

To the town of Pine Mountain, Georgia—
where the trees stand tall,
and the past whispers in the wind.
May the spirit of this place continue to
inspire stories, both told and untold.

Table of Contents

Welcome to
Pine Hollow

Pine Hollow is a town of secrets, where the fog rolls in like a shroud, and the pines stand tall, silent witnesses to the passage of time. A place where people don't ask questions, and history stays buried beneath the rustling leaves of the forest floor.

Sloane Wren thought she'd left this small town behind—along with the mysteries that haunted it. But when her father, a retired detective, falls ill, she returns to Pine Hollow, drawn back to the very place she tried to forget.

What she doesn't know is that Pine Hollow has been waiting. And its secrets are far darker than she could ever imagine..

Chapter 1
The Empty Chalet

S loane Wren had never liked the sound of a cabin in the woods.

Not the hoot of owls or the whisper of wind through pine needles. Not even the soft lap of water against the lake's shore. It was the silence that came afterward. The thick, unnatural kind that seemed to settle between the trees and watch you.

The kind that filled Cabin 17.

The lock gave way with a reluctant click, and she pushed the door open with her shoulder. It scraped against the uneven floorboards, just as it had when she was a kid. That hadn't changed. The smell hit her next— pine wood, old dust, a hint of mildew, and something harder to place. Something like time itself.

She stepped inside and let the door close behind her.

It was exactly as she remembered.

The cabin was small, a two-room layout with a narrow kitchen, a cramped bathroom, and a single bedroom in the back. The living area took up most of the space, anchored by a stone fireplace and a battered recliner that had long ago molded itself to her father's shape. The same wool blanket still hung over the arm, the one her mother used to knit during long winters, before she passed.

Sloane ran her fingers along the back of the recliner. The fabric was more threadbare than she remembered, but the feel of it brought back the image of Jack Wren in his prime—leaning forward in that very chair, eyes sharp, voice low, solving murders in cities that never knew his name. Back when he was more legend than man.

She crossed to the small built-in bookshelf beside the fireplace. Most of the paperbacks were true crime. A few of her own novels were tucked between them—likely placed there by her father when she wasn't looking, always pretending he didn't read them, never admitting he was proud.

Her gaze drifted to a small wooden box sitting on the top shelf. She pulled it down and opened it, the hinges creaking like something out of one of her stories. Inside was his badge—Pine Hollow PD, Detective Jack Wren, tarnished but intact.

She held it in her palm for a long time.

He'd always kept it close, even after he retired. It was more than a symbol. It was the part of him that hadn't been touched by forgetting. The one thing dementia hadn't yet stolen. When he held it, he still stood a little straighter.

Sloane set the badge gently back into the box and exhaled through her nose.

"Still the hero, huh, Dad?" she murmured.

Her eyes landed on the floorboards just beneath the window. One of them was darker than the others, warped ever so slightly in the middle. The crawlspace. She remembered hiding toys down there as a child, giggling while her father pretended not to notice. But when she came back last spring, just before the diagnosis, he'd stopped her mid-step.

"Don't go in there, Sloane," he'd said, his voice hollow. *"Some things need to stay buried."*

At the time she'd thought it was just confusion. Now she wasn't so sure.

She knelt down, brushed away the dust, and ran her fingers along the edge of the plank. It was loose. She pried it up with a soft creak, revealing a shallow space beneath—barely big enough for a child to crawl through.

But there was something tucked inside. Something wedged between the crossbeams. She reached in and carefully pulled it free.

A folded piece of yellowed newspaper.

She unfolded it slowly, and the image that stared back at her sent a chill down her spine.

A girl. Blonde. Smiling wide, the kind of summer photo that belonged in a yearbook.

Delia Reese.

The headline read:

Missing Since July 12, 1995 –
Last Seen in Cabin 9.

Sloane swallowed hard.

She remembered the whispers. Delia's name had lived in Pine Hollow longer than some of the residents. The girl who vanished without a trace. The one no one ever talked about unless they'd had a few drinks and were looking to scare a newcomer.

But the clipping wasn't from some random local collector. It was hidden. Buried. Left intentionally.

And it was in her father's cabin.

Outside, gravel crunched under slow-moving footsteps.

She moved quickly to the window and peered through the curtain.

A man stood just beyond the property line, arms crossed. Watching the cabin with quiet intensity.

Sloane didn't recognize him at first. Tall, broad-shouldered, and unshaven. Then she remembered the boat dock manager her father had mentioned in passing—Caleb Foster.

The man from Cabin 16.

He turned, locked eyes with her for just a second, then walked away, disappearing into the trees.

Sloane let the curtain fall back into place.

Whatever she'd just uncovered, someone else already knew it was here.

And Pine Hollow wasn't going to stay quiet for long.

Chapter 2
Ashes and Embers

Sloane stood in the middle of Cabin 17, the newspaper clipping still in her hand, her fingers creasing the edges as if she could squeeze answers from the ink.

Outside, the lake whispered, and wind stirred the pines like a breath through dry bones.

She tucked the clipping into her notebook and slid it onto the shelf behind a row of old books. Later. She'd look at it again later, when her mind was clearer.

For now, there was someone else she needed to see.

She stepped onto the back porch, where the wood had gone soft under years of damp. The path that led to the caretaker's cabin was short—just a slow bend around the trees and past the old garden where her mother used to grow herbs and tomatoes in rusted cans. Nothing grew there now but moss and memory.

The caretaker's cabin had once been a tool shed. Her father had turned it into a kind of retreat for himself after retirement—before the forgetting began. Before he stopped recognizing his neighbors. Before he started asking about her mother like she might come home any minute.

She knocked twice on the frame and pushed the door open gently.

"Dad?"

The small space was warm. A single lamp glowed in the corner, and the air smelled like cinnamon and dust. Jack Wren sat in a high-backed chair by the window, his eyes fixed on the lake through the smeared glass. A flannel blanket was draped over his knees. The badge box she'd held earlier now rested on the table beside him, open like a shrine.

"Hey," she said softly, moving closer. "You warm enough?"

He didn't look at her at first. Then his gaze shifted, slow as honey.

His face brightened. "Sloane."

He reached for her hand, and she let him take it.

"You came," he said, as if this were the first time he'd seen her in years. "I was wondering if you would."

She smiled, even though her heart clenched a little tighter every time he forgot. "Of course I did. I'm staying a while, remember? Taking care of things."

He nodded, still holding her hand. "I knew you'd come. Always said you had your mother's spine."

Sloane pulled up a wooden stool and sat beside him. "How are you feeling today?"

He scratched his cheek. "Some days are better than others." Then, after a pause: "You see anything strange in the house?"

The question was too pointed. Her heart skipped a beat.

"Strange how?"

"I don't know," he said, voice quieter. "Sometimes I think it watches."

Sloane blinked. "What watches?"

Jack's brow furrowed. He looked out the window again, then shook his head. "Not important."

"Dad…"

"Cabin 9," he muttered. "That's where it started. We never should've touched it. I told them that."

Her breath caught.

He rubbed his temples and sat back. "But they didn't listen. No one ever listens."

She leaned in. "Are you talking about Delia Reese?"

His hand twitched, like the name had shocked him.

"Birdie knew," he whispered. "They all knew. Covered it up, built new stories over the bones. The Association wanted it buried."

Sloane's pulse thudded in her ears. "Who's *they*, Dad?"

But he only stared back at her, blank and soft-eyed like the moment had vanished.

"Did you bring any tea?" he asked. "It's chilly tonight."

She nodded slowly. "Yeah. I'll make some."

She rose, squeezing his shoulder gently before stepping back outside. The door clicked behind her, and she stood on the porch a moment, letting the wind hit her face.

Birdie knew.

They built new stories over the bones.

Her father wasn't making sense, not completely—but there was a pattern in his ramblings. He always circled the same names. Delia. Birdie. The Association. Cabin 9.

She turned back toward Cabin 17, but movement between the trees made her pause.

Caleb Foster stood at the tree line again, a black hoodie pulled over his head. He wasn't looking at her this time—he was staring at the lake, arms folded tight across his chest.

He hadn't made a sound.

Sloane hesitated, then stepped off the porch.

"Hey," she called. "You're Caleb, right?"

He turned, met her eyes. His face was unreadable—tired, maybe. Guarded.

"Yeah."

"You were outside earlier. Watching the cabin."

He raised an eyebrow. "I was walking to the dock. Your place just happens to be on the way."

"You always stop and stare?"

"I do when someone's snooping around places that should've stayed quiet."

Sloane stepped closer, voice firm. "What does that mean?"

Caleb tilted his head. "You've been in that cabin five minutes and you're already stirring dust better left settled."

"You mean Cabin 17?"

Her eyes narrowed. "Or are you talking about Cabin 9?"

His expression shifted—but just for a second. A flicker of something behind his eyes. He looked away, then back again, his jaw tight.

"I don't know nothing about Cabin Nine," he said slowly, like each word had been weighed and chosen for survival.

Then, softer, leaning in: "And you need to know… she never should've been there alone."

His gaze locked on hers. "And neither should you."

Sloane felt a cold breath roll through her, like the trees had whispered something too.

By the time she found her voice, he was already gone—vanishing back into the shadows of the trail, leaving the silence behind him heavier than it had been before.

Chapter 3
Don't Ask Questions

The sun had barely cracked through the morning clouds by the time Sloane made her way down the winding gravel road toward town. Pine Hollow didn't so much *wake up* as it quietly resumed existing, like it had never truly slept.

She walked past scattered cabins—some looked lived-in, with rocking chairs and wind chimes, while others sat like silent watchers, their windows dark, their porches bowed with age. Cabin 9 was just ahead, tucked slightly off the main road like it didn't want to be seen.

Sloane kept walking, Caleb's words about Cabin 9 still echoing in her head.

The one-street town came into view slowly, almost shyly. The Old Hollow Bakery, Marla's Treasures & Trinkets, a hardware store that didn't seem to have updated its inventory since the late '90s. A handful of weathered benches lined the sidewalk, flanked by patchy flowerbeds and rusted signs from seasonal festivals long past.

Sloane stepped into the bakery, the little brass bell above the door jingling like something out of a Hallmark movie.

The scent hit her instantly—warm cinnamon, coffee, and sugar, with a hint of lavender and something yeasty rising from the ovens in back.

"Morning," came a voice from behind the counter.

Birdie Dupree was exactly how she remembered her: thick-framed glasses on a chain around her neck, a gray bun twisted into something solid, and an apron that looked older than Sloane. Her smile was polite— but not welcoming.

"Well I'll be," Birdie said, a gentle southern lilt coloring her words. "If it ain't little Sloane Wren. Thought you were done with this ol' place."

"For a while," Sloane replied, moving toward the counter. "Looking after my dad now."

Birdie's smile didn't waver, but her eyes narrowed just a touch. "He's still got some fight in him, that one. Shame what happened to his mind."

Sloane gave a nod, pretending it didn't sting. "Yeah. It's been rough."

Birdie turned to grab a cinnamon roll from the case. "So. You writin' a new book while you're here? Plenty of inspiration in these parts."

"Actually," Sloane said, leaning slightly on the counter, "I came across an old article. About a girl who went missing here in '95. Delia Reese."

Birdie paused—barely. But Sloane noticed it. Her hands moved slower, more deliberate.

"That was a long time ago," Birdie said lightly. "Terrible business. Folks still whisper it now and then, though I don't know what good it does."

"She disappeared from Cabin 9, right?"

Birdie's eyes lifted, calm but sharp.

"Some cabins don't like to be remembered, sugar."

Sloane blinked. "Excuse me?"

Birdie wrapped the cinnamon roll in wax paper and handed it across the counter. "Sometimes, the best thing you can do is leave old ghosts where they lay. Pine Hollow's got its own rhythm. Folks 'round here are... protective."

Sloane didn't move. "Protective of what?"

Birdie smiled again, cool and sugar-sweet. "Its own, sugar. Pine Hollow protects its own."

Sloane left a generous tip on the table and, without another word, walked out the door.

———

She crossed the street to Marla's Treasures, still holding the untouched cinnamon roll. The shop was cluttered with antique furniture, vinyl records, and an endless collection of dusty books no one had alphabetized.

Marla herself was dozing behind the counter, a tabby cat curled in her lap.

Sloane wandered toward the back, toward the haphazard stacks of old magazines and local newsletters. After a few minutes of digging, she found what she was looking for: a Pine Hollow High School yearbook from 1995. The spine was cracked, the gold foil on the cover faded.

She flipped through quickly, and there she was—Delia Reese, senior, varsity tennis, debate club, and "Most Likely to Leave Town and Never Look Back."

Sloane stared at her smiling face, that same one from the newspaper clipping. Confident. Sharp. Alive.

She scanned the pages, looking for other names that stood out—Bryce Walden, Tina Lomax, Derrick Myles—all listed next to her in various clubs and group photos. She tore a scrap of paper from her notebook and made a list.

Maybe someone still lived in town.

She snapped a photo of Delia's picture on her phone, just as the bell above the shop door jingled.

She waited, listening. No footsteps. Just the soft creak of the door closing behind someone.

Sloane poked her head out from the aisle.

No one was there.

———

On her way back to the cabin, she took the long route—the one that passed Cabin 9.

She didn't stop. Didn't even slow her pace.

But her eyes locked on the warped wooden steps, the way the porch sagged just a little more than it should've. A faded wind chime hung above the door, tangled and still, despite the breeze. The cabin looked... *wrong*. Like it was holding its breath.

And Sloane could swear—swear on her life—that one of the windows was open just a crack.

Like someone inside wanted to hear.

Chapter 4
Not One of Us

The names from the yearbook burned a hole in her notebook all morning.

Bryce Walden, Derrick Myles, Tina Lomax.

Delia's classmates. People who might remember something—*anything*. She'd looked them up online the night before, digging through local business directories and social media posts. Most were long gone from Pine Hollow.

Except Tina.

Tina Lomax Styles, according to the hand-painted sign out front—a curling script in chipped gold on a sun-bleached board above a narrow, peach-colored salon. Faded curtains sagged in the front windows, their seams yellowed with time.

Sloane stepped inside, the bell above the door giving a lazy jingle.

The scent of hairspray hit her first, layered over dryer heat and something vaguely floral—lavender, maybe. The walls were painted coral, though age had dulled it to a dusty rose. Old gossip magazines curled on the waiting bench like neglected houseplants.

From behind a low divider, a voice called, "Be with you in just a sec!"

Sloane browsed a wall of framed snapshots—bridal hairdos, prom curls, pageant waves. Tina was in many of them, her smile warm but wary, like she didn't quite trust the camera.

When Tina finally appeared, she had a towel over one shoulder and a smudge of dye near her temple. Her eyes swept over Sloane and widened with recognition.

"Well I'll be," she said, her accent soft and syrupy. "If it ain't Jack Wren's girl. I almost didn't recognize you."

Sloane smiled. "It's been a while."

"I'd say so. You were here what—just the summer before college?"

"Three months."

Tina nodded slowly, folding the towel. "Folks were sure your daddy'd settle down here for good. But you… you always looked like you were passin' through."

Sloane let the comment hang.

"I came back to help out," she said. "His memory's not what it used to be."

Tina gave a sympathetic hum. "Shame, that. He was sharp. Always liked your daddy. Real presence about him."

Sloane hesitated. "I was wondering if I could ask you about someone."

"Oh?" Tina reached for a comb but didn't use it. "You doin' research for a book?"

"Something like that." Sloane opened her notebook. "Delia Reese."

Tina stilled, her smile fixed in place.

Sloane pressed. "You two were in the same class, right?"

"That was a long time ago," Tina said slowly. "Terrible thing. Never really got over it, truth be told."

"She disappeared from Cabin 9?"

Tina's eyes narrowed just slightly. "So they say."

Just like that Tina's countenance changed, she smiled like they'd just been talking about the weather. "You need anything trimmed up while you're here? Or just passing through?"

And that was it. The door closed again.

Sloane smiled, thanked her, and left a business card on the counter—"just in case something comes to mind."

She knew Tina wouldn't call.

———

But when Tina turned back, she smiled like they'd just been talking about the weather. "You need anything trimmed up while you're here? Or just passing through?"

And that was it. The door closed again.

Sloane smiled, thanked her, and left a business card on the counter—"just in case something comes to mind."

She knew Tina wouldn't call.

———

Back at Cabin 17, the light was changing—soft and gold, with long shadows stretching through the trees like reaching arms.

She poured a cup of coffee, sat by the front window, and stared out toward the bend in the gravel road.

Cabin 9 was just barely visible. A dark shape between the trees.

She hadn't stopped that morning when she passed it. Caleb's warning still rang too fresh in her ears.

But now... the curiosity pressed at her like a hand between her shoulder blades.

She slipped into her jacket and stepped outside.

———

The trees lining the path seemed taller here. Closer together. The air was cooler—not cold, exactly, but thinner somehow, like there was less oxygen near Cabin 9.

The structure itself looked like the others: wood siding, small porch, moss-covered shingles.

But something about it resisted light.

Even in the late-day sun, shadows clung to the roofline and pooled beneath the steps. Vines crawled up the foundation like they were trying to drag the whole place back underground.

Sloane slowed at the foot of the porch. The wind chime hanging near the door was tangled with dead leaves, unmoving.

She stepped onto the bottom step.

The wood moaned like it hadn't been touched in years.

She stared at the door—painted red once, now dulled to rust. The windows were streaked, but not dirty. Just... blurred. Like the glass was sweating from the inside.

Her eyes locked on the doorknob. Brass, discolored. Old, but not untouched.

And there—just beneath it—scratches. Tiny, jagged ones. Like fingernails had scraped at the wood.

She stepped back, breath catching.

The air here didn't move. No birdsong. No breeze. Even the trees seemed to lean away from the cabin, as if afraid to touch it.

Sloane backed off the porch and returned to the road with her pulse thudding in her ears.

———

Back at Cabin 17, dusk had fallen hard.

She set her notebook on the table and turned on the lamp. Warm light bloomed across the walls, but it didn't chase away the chill she brought back with her.

She unzipped her jacket and froze.

There, on her pillow, sat a folded piece of paper.

Her breath stopped.

She stepped closer, slowly, as if approaching a wild animal.

The paper was crisp. White. Folded once.

She opened it.

One word.
Scrawled in a crooked hand:

Stop.

Chapter 5
Echoes in the Walls

The word was still sitting in her hand.

Stop.

Not in all caps. Not scribbled like a threat. Just… written. Calm. Shaky. Like someone had sat down, folded a piece of paper, and left her a polite warning.

But there was nothing polite about it.

Sloane stood in the center of the room, pulse in her ears, the lamp throwing long, uneven shadows across the walls. The air inside the cabin had shifted—something about it felt tighter now. More aware.

She checked the windows. Locked.

The doors. Deadbolted.

No footprints on the porch, no broken screens, no sign of entry. But that didn't mean anything. Whoever left it hadn't needed to break in. They belonged here.

She sat on the edge of the bed, the paper still between her fingers, and looked around the room. Cabin 17 was silent, but it was the kind of silence that had weight to it. The kind that held its breath.

She folded the note back in half and slipped it into her notebook behind the clipping of Delia.

Then she stood, grabbed her flashlight, and walked out into the dark.

———

The caretaker's cabin was just down the path, tucked behind the trees. Moonlight broke through the canopy in thin slices, brushing silver across pine needles and damp earth. Her boots crunched softly on gravel.

She didn't knock.

"Dad?"

Jack Wren was seated in his usual chair, staring out the window like he was waiting for something to emerge from the lake.

He didn't turn when she entered.

"Dad, did someone come into my cabin tonight?"

No answer.

"Did you let someone in?"

He blinked, slow. "You hear the wind talking again?"

She knelt beside him, flashlight resting on her knee. "Someone left me a note. One word: *stop*."

That got his attention.

His head turned. Not fast—but purposeful.

"You found it."

Sloane froze. "Found what?"

Jack stared at her like he didn't recognize her, then like he did, but wished he didn't.

"The girl," he murmured. "You're walking her path."

Sloane's throat tightened. "You mean Delia?"

He looked away.

"She came around asking questions, too. Digging where she shouldn't. Cabin Nine showed her something, and that was the end of it."

"You said you told them to leave it alone," she pressed. "Who's *them*, Dad? Who was she talking to?"

Jack's eyes watered. His hand trembled on the armrest. "Birdie knew. And Ray Lomax. And the Walden boy. They made sure it stayed quiet."

"Made sure how?"

He looked at her, and for a moment, she saw her father again—not the confused, fading version—but the detective. The man who used to see straight through a lie.

"They erased her," he said, barely above a whisper.

Sloane swallowed. "But she didn't vanish."

"No," he said. "She was taken."

Her blood turned to ice.

Jack leaned forward suddenly, grabbing her wrist with surprising strength.

"You've gotta be careful," he rasped. "They think you're just the daughter. That you'll go home when you hit a wall. But if you don't…"

His eyes searched hers.

"They'll make you disappear, too."

———

Sloane left the caretaker's cabin shaken, Jack's words echoing in her head as she made her way back up the path. The trees around her seemed taller than they had before—looming, closing in.

As she neared her own porch, something caught her eye.

Movement.

She turned her flashlight sharply—aimed it toward the edge of the woods.

Nothing.

She waited.

Branches shifted. A breath of wind—or something else.

She backed toward the cabin, keys in hand.

Once inside, she locked every door and drew the curtains. The floor creaked beneath her feet like it remembered someone else's steps.

She didn't sleep that night.

———

By sunrise, she had made her decision.

She opened her notebook and stared at the list of names. Bryce was long gone. Tina had said her piece—or refused to. That left one name circled in red ink.

Derrick Myles.

According to a post in a local contractor Facebook group, he still lived just outside of town. Ran a small business fixing up cabins for the Association.

If anyone knew which ones had been... tampered with, it was him.

Sloane took a breath and underlined his name twice.

Chapter 6
Splinters Beneath the Paint

It took Sloane half the morning to find the right gravel road.

Derrick Myles didn't exactly advertise—his name wasn't on the side of his truck, and his Facebook page hadn't been updated in two years—but a comment on a local message board said he was "working up near Old Elk Road," refitting one of the lakeside cabins for the Association.

Cabin 22, according to a crooked wooden placard nailed to a tree.

The air felt different this far from town—denser. The forest was thicker, as if the trees leaned in to listen. Less maintained. Less watched.

She parked a short distance back and followed the path on foot, boots crunching through wet leaves and pine needles.

The sound of hammering broke the quiet. Steady. Focused.

She rounded a bend and found him.

Derrick Myles was taller than she remembered—thick arms, shaved head, deep tan lines at his neck. He crouched beside the cabin, hammering a warped floorboard into place, his shirt stained with sweat and sawdust. His toolbelt clinked with every shift.

Sloane stepped forward carefully. "Derrick?"

He glanced up, squinting. "Yeah?"

"I'm Sloane Wren. Jack's daughter."

He stood slowly, brushing dust from his jeans, his eyes narrowing just slightly.

"I remember you," he said. "You were just a kid."

"I'm back now. Looking after him."

He nodded. Neutral. Guarded.

"I was hoping to ask you something," she said. "About Delia Reese."

The name turned the air still.

He scanned the tree line behind her before answering. "I don't talk about that."

"I'm not here to stir things up," Sloane said gently. "I just want to understand what happened. You were part of the maintenance crew back then, right?"

Silence. Then: "I worked on Cabin 9. Before she vanished."

"What do you think happened?"

Derrick grabbed a bottle of water from a cooler, cracked it open, took a long drink. His hand trembled faintly as he recapped it.

"She asked too many questions. About the wrong people."

"Who?"

"She thought the cabins weren't just cabins. Said there was a system. Tunnels, markers. Said there were more than a hundred of them, but only a few were registered."

Sloane raised her brows. "Are there?"

He stared at her, then held up five fingers.

"That's it. The rest are private. Legacy properties. Built by people who don't want them tied to public records."

"Why?"

Instead of answering, he nodded toward the side of the cabin.

"You want to know where it started? Look beneath the siding."

Sloane crouched beside the wall and gently pulled back a warped plank. Beneath it, the wood was older—rough, gray with age—but still firm. And carved deep into the grain, almost lost in the weathering, was a symbol.

A circle.

And inside it—a bird in flight. Small. Sleek. Crest tilted, wings swept back like blades.

Not just any bird.

A Pine Siskin. The town's official bird. Printed on the welcome sign, etched into city hall stationery. Friendly. Familiar.

But here, carved into hidden wood, it felt different. Like a sigil. Like a warning.

The edges of the carving had been singed. Someone had tried to burn it out.

Sloane ran her fingers over the charred grooves. "What is this?"

Derrick still didn't look at her. "You know what it is."

"It's the town's bird."

"It's *their* mark."

"The Association?"

He gave a slow nod.

"The Founders. The old families. You see that symbol, you know who built it. Who owns it. Who keeps it quiet."

Sloane stood slowly, brushing dirt from her hands. "Why would they mark a cabin?"

He finally met her eyes.

"They don't mark cabins, Miss Wren. They mark people. Ideas. Secrets. Things they want kept in the ground."

She swallowed. "So why was Delia looking?"

"Because she thought the cabins were talking to each other."

Sloane frowned. "What does that mean?"

"She said they were connected," Derrick muttered. "Underneath. Like roots. She said they remembered things. Things that happened inside them."

"And you?"

"I think she wasn't entirely wrong."

A silence fell between them, dense as the woods.

"You keep pullin' threads," he said, voice lower now, "and this whole place'll unravel. You might not like what's underneath."

Sloane looked back at the carved Pine Siskin in the wood—its wings spread in motion, its eye forever open.

And for the first time since returning to Pine Hollow, she felt like something was watching her back.

Chapter 7
The Ones Who Built This Place

The Pine Siskin wouldn't leave her head.

Not the bird itself—the real finch was harmless enough. But the one carved beneath the siding of Cabin 22… that bird had looked alive. Watching. Branded into the wood like it had grown there.

Sloane drove back to town with the windows down, hoping the chill in the air would clear the heaviness from her chest. It didn't.

She parked near the bakery and sat for a moment, fingers tight on the steering wheel, watching people drift in and out of the little shops like everything was normal.

And maybe it was—for them.

But now, everywhere she looked, she saw it.

The same symbol.

A circle. A bird in flight.

Faded into the corner of the bakery's chalkboard sign, barely visible beneath a daily special.

Etched into the cast-iron bench in front of town hall—one wing just chipped enough to go unnoticed.

Stamped into the wax seal of a town council bulletin on the corkboard outside the hardware store.

It was *everywhere*.

She stepped out of the car, heart picking up speed.

———

Inside the bakery, warmth hit her like a wave—coffee, sugar, and cinnamon all melting into a cloud that smelled like childhood.

Birdie stood behind the counter, her expression neutral, her apron smeared with flour.

"Well hey there," she said, dusting her hands. "Back so soon?"

Sloane nodded, stepping up to the counter. "Came for another cinnamon roll."

Birdie slid one into a paper sleeve and passed it over. "And here I thought you were just visitin'."

"I am. Sort of."

Birdie tilted her head. "Funny thing, that. You grow up here— even for a little while—and folks remember. But leave too long…" She shrugged. "Pine Hollow forgets you right back."

Sloane leaned against the counter. "What about the people who *want* to be forgotten?"

Birdie's eyes sharpened. "Now what would make you say somethin' like that?"

"I saw the bird symbol," Sloane said, quiet but steady. "Carved into a cabin. Burned into the wood."

Birdie didn't move for a second. Then she exhaled softly and began wiping down the counter again.

"You should mind where you're lookin', sugar."

"I think Delia saw it too."

Birdie stopped.

"That girl…" she said, shaking her head. "She was too smart for her own good. Thought if she asked enough questions, she could make Pine Hollow give her answers."

Sloane's throat tightened. "What happened to her?"

Birdie's voice softened—low, almost sweet. "Some people get told to stop. Others get shown."

A pause.

"She kept going."

The words fell between them like a stone dropped into deep water.

Sloane swallowed. "And if I don't stop?"

Birdie stared her in the eyes.
A stare that spoke louder than any word could.

Sloane backed away toward the door, her pulse thudding in her throat.

Birdie, back to her usual sweet southern tone, said brightly, "You have a blessed day, sugar."

<hr>

Outside, the clouds had thickened—gray and low, like the sky was pressing down on the town.

Sloane wandered down the street and turned onto a narrow side road that led to the back of the Pine Hollow Historical Hall, where the original founding documents had been displayed for decades behind glass cases and dust.

The building smelled of wood polish and forgotten secrets.

Inside, it was empty—except for a small desk with a guestbook, and a row of framed charters lining the far wall.

And there it was.

On the earliest blueprint of Pine Hollow's original resort plan—a faded sheet of parchment from 1952:

The Pine Siskin.

Centered in a perfect circle. Stylized, elegant, its wings outstretched, head lifted like a crown.

Labeled underneath in elegant script:

"For the protection and preservation of Pine Hollow—The Founders' Mark."

She stared at it, her reflection warped in the glass.

They hadn't just left their mark on the cabins.

They'd stamped it into the town's foundation.

Chapter 8
The Ones Who Stay Quiet

The wind picked up just after dark.

It howled down from the ridge, rattling the branches and whispering through the trees like something alive. A storm was coming, but Sloane didn't care.

She was going back to Cabin 9.

No more standing on the porch. No more staring through the window. No more pretending she hadn't seen the symbol, or heard the warnings, or watched her father flinch at Delia's name.

She pulled on her jacket, stuffed a flashlight and prybar into her bag, and locked the door behind her.

The gravel crunched loud beneath her boots, but only for a few steps. Then it was pine needles and packed dirt—the kind of ground that didn't echo back. The forest felt thicker than before. Closer.

Cabin 9 appeared through the trees like it had been waiting for her.

The wind had scattered leaves across the porch, collecting in dry curls along the steps. The warped railing sagged, and the windows stared out like blank eyes.

She climbed the steps slowly. Every board creaked, as if protesting her presence.

The door didn't budge at first. She tried the handle—locked. She knelt, felt under the edge of the porch, and found what she'd hoped: a rusted key tucked inside a crack in the foundation.

Small towns were creatures of habit.

She slipped it into the lock and turned.

It opened.

———

The air inside was thick with mildew and age. The smell of damp wood and something older—like dust and memory and things meant to be forgotten. She swept her flashlight in a slow arc.

The cabin was bare.

A broken armchair in one corner. A warped bookshelf, its contents long gone. Cobwebs framed the window like lace. The walls were a dirty, sun-faded green, the floor scratched and splintered.

Sloane stepped inside, the door creaking shut behind her.

The silence wasn't empty—it was *watchful*.

She moved carefully, sweeping the light across the floor, the walls, the ceiling. Her beam caught something near the fireplace—a shape etched into the wall.

She crouched.

A name. Carved in uneven letters.

D. Reese.

Beneath it: "It watches."

Her breath caught.

The flashlight flickered.

She smacked the side of it. It steadied.

She backed away and moved toward the back room—the bedroom. The door stuck, swollen in its frame, but gave way with a groan.

Inside: dust, wallpaper peeling at the corners, an old mattress stripped to its frame. Nothing else.

Until she noticed the floor.

One board was looser than the others.

She dropped to her knees, slid the prybar from her bag, and wedged it beneath the edge. With a soft crack, the board lifted.

Beneath it—nothing at first. Just a dark, shallow hollow.

Then she saw it.

The Pine Siskin. Carved clean into the subfloor. No burn marks this time. Just the bird, inside a perfect circle.

She touched it.

The air shifted. Cold. Sharp.

And then—a sound.

From behind her.

Not footsteps. Not wind.

Breathing.

She froze.

Turned.

Nothing.

But outside—through the streaked bedroom window—she saw it.

A figure.

Standing just beyond the tree line. Too far to see clearly. But standing. Watching.

She killed her flashlight.

The cabin sank into darkness.

By the time she looked again, the figure was gone.

She left the way she came, quickly but carefully, locking the door behind her with trembling hands. The wind had died. The woods were still.

Too still.

———

Back at Cabin 17, she locked every door and didn't turn on a single light.

She sat at the table, notebook open, heart racing, staring down at what she'd written:

Σ Delia's name carved inside.

Σ "It watches."

Σ Pine Siskin under the floorboard.

Σ Someone was outside.

They hadn't stopped her.

But they knew she was there.

And now she knew they were watching, too.

Chapter 9
The Page That Shouldn't Exist

The morning after Cabin 9, Sloane didn't move for a long time.

She sat curled on the edge of her bed, notebook open, the silence of Cabin 17 stretching long and taut around her. The floor creaked now and then. The trees whispered. She didn't know if the figure she saw had been real—but something had been there.

And someone had been in that cabin before her.

Delia.

Her name had been carved into the wall, her warning burned into the floor.

It watches.

Sloane had the creeping feeling Delia had been leaving a trail—one piece at a time. Not for the town. Not for the sheriff. For someone like Sloane.

She needed to go where the town wouldn't expect her to look.

So she went to the library.

Pine Hollow's public library sat just off Main Street, tucked behind a crumbling stone church and a row of maples that had already begun to bleed gold.

The inside hadn't changed since the late '90s—laminate floors, pale green paint, and the faint, musty scent of aging paper and tired fluorescent bulbs.

Sloane walked straight past the new arrivals shelf and headed to the back—Archives. A narrow room lined with file cabinets, high school yearbooks, old newsletters, and boxes marked with handwritten labels.

She started with the summer of 1995.

Nothing in the newsletters. Nothing in the microfilm—just the same article she already had, the same official story: *Delia Reese, 18, missing. No leads. Last seen near Cabin 9.*

But there was something strange in the "Miscellaneous Submissions" file from that fall.

Tucked between a poem about the changing leaves and a notice for the Fall Founders Festival was a thin envelope, unmarked, sealed in plastic.

Inside was a single handwritten page.

The handwriting was jagged, rushed. Black ink on yellowing notebook paper.

Sloane unfolded it with trembling fingers and read:

———

September 5th, 1995

If you're reading this, you're already too close.
I tried to tell someone. RW said not to. Said it would blow back on me. I think he's right.

There's something under the cabins. I don't know if it's tunnels, or if it's just how they're all connected. But I've been hearing things—

Voices, when the wind passes through the boards. Footsteps when I'm the only one inside.

I found the mark under Cabin 3. Same one on the Association letters. The bird in the circle.

They say it's the town's bird. But it's not a symbol of pride. It's a seal.
Like the branding of cattle—a warning that this doesn't belong to you. To stay away.

If something happens to me—look in the floorboards. Not just in 9. Others too. I think they're hiding records. Maybe people. I don't know.

But I'm going to Cabin 0 tonight. I found a path behind the chapel. I'll leave another page if I can.

—D

———

Sloane stared at the signature.

—D.

No last name.

No mention of Delia.

But the reference to the symbol... the cabins... *Cabin 0*... it was her. It had to be her.

She turned the page over. Nothing on the back.

But in the bottom corner, faint and almost missed, was a stamp in red ink:

Property of Pine Hollow Preservation Society.

She had never heard of it.

And yet... it felt familiar. Too familiar.

She traced the corner with her finger and whispered aloud, "RW."

Birdie had mentioned Ray Lomax once—someone from her father's old circle. He was gone now. Dead two years, buried behind the church where the trail to Cabin 0 supposedly began.

Which meant whoever Delia was afraid of...

Was still here.

Chapter 10
The Missing Cabin

Sloane sat at the kitchen table of Cabin 17, Jack's old hand-drawn map spread across her notebooks like a puzzle no one ever finished. Each line, each numbered box had been carefully drawn, labeled, and highlighted—Cabins 1 through 100.

But no zero.

She flipped through a laminated brochure from the drawer, rubbed the faded cover between her fingers. Same layout. Same numbers. A perfect little grid of cabins and dirt paths.

"No zero," she murmured.

And yet Delia had written it down in her note.

Cabin 0. I found a path behind the chapel…

If it existed, someone had gone out of their way to erase it.

She needed a place the town wouldn't expect her to look.

So she went to the Pine Hollow Preservation Society.

The Preservation Society's headquarters was housed in an old brick schoolhouse on the edge of town, tucked between a row of maple trees and the rust-stained chapel. The building had settled into the landscape like a tombstone—weathered, watchful, and unmoved by time.

Inside, the air smelled like lemon polish, brittle paper, and lavender gone a little sour. A bell chimed gently above the door as she stepped inside.

"Afternoon," said the woman at the front desk—sixties, stern bun, glasses strung on a jeweled chain. "Help you find somethin', hon?"

"I'm doing some research," Sloane said. "On the original resort development. Old maps, if you have them."

The woman tilted her head, just slightly. "That depend on who's askin'."

Sloane gave her best polite, harmless smile. "Just a writer. Family's been here a long time."

The woman nodded. "East wing. Third cabinet. Keep the drawers neat."

The archive room was colder than the rest of the building, lit by tall windows and a single flickering fluorescent bulb that buzzed like a fly trapped in a jar. Metal file cabinets lined the walls, their drawers dented and labeled by decade. Dust floated in lazy spirals through the shafts of sun, and the air buzzed faintly with the hum of something older than electricity.

Sloane rolled up her sleeves and got to work.

She started in the 1950s, then the '60s. Plat maps, zoning documents, tax ledgers, deed logs. She pulled one after the other, spreading them across the wide oak table.

Cabins 1 through 100.

No mention of a zero.

She checked land surveys. Permits. Even an old hand-drawn elevation plan with coffee stains across half the paper.

Nothing.

She moved on to the '80s. The '90s. Still nothing. Time slipped past in dusty page after dusty page. Her eyes blurred. Her shoulders ached.

An hour. Maybe two.

She stood, rubbing the back of her neck, and wandered the room—half from exhaustion, half from frustration. The light had shifted while she searched; the late afternoon sun now poured in through the tall windows in golden slants that dust danced through.

She paced near the far wall, trailing her fingers along the wainscoting, barely looking anymore.

And then—a glint.

A sharp gleam of light reflected into her eyes—just a flicker—but enough to stop her.

She turned.

A frame on the wall had caught the sun.

It was a large display map, mounted behind glass and slightly crooked in its frame. The top read.
"Wildlife Habitats of Pine Hollow   1987 Community Stewardship Project."

She stepped closer.

The map was newer than the plats, but not digital. Faded greens and blues marked wooded zones and wildlife corridors, with hand-drawn notations pointing out trails and birdwatching sites.

At first glance, it looked like nothing.

But then she saw it.

Near the bottom left corner—just behind the chapel, where the town map showed nothing but forest—a stamped emblem had been superimposed onto the terrain.

Not labeled. Not explained.

Just sitting there.

A circle.
A Pine Siskin.
Wings flared. Head raised. Talons extended.

The same mark she'd found burned into cabin wood, hidden beneath siding, carved under floorboards.

It was on the town's stationery. Their welcome signs.

But here, it was alone. Floating on the map with no legend, no number, no context.

And right where Delia said Cabin 0 would be.

Sloane leaned in until her breath fogged the glass.

It hadn't been listed.

It had been sealed.

Like a wound.

———

She took a photo with her phone, then stepped back, heart pounding. The gleam of light that had drawn her in had already shifted, as if it had only revealed the truth for a moment.

Almost like it had wanted her to find it.

———

Back in her car, she spread out the notes and maps on the passenger seat.

The coordinates placed it just beyond the back edge of the church cemetery, where the trail forked behind the old garden wall.

Delia had found it. She'd gone there.

Now Sloane would, too.

Chapter 11
The One That Wasn't
Supposed to Be Found

The trail behind the chapel was more suggestion than path.

At one time, it might've been used regularly—by groundskeepers, churchgoers, maybe the curious—but time had erased most of it. Brambles clawed at her jeans. Moss slicked the earth beneath her boots. Every branch she pushed aside sprang back behind her like it wanted to seal the way shut.

Sloane pressed on, flashlight tucked into her jacket pocket, a chill spidering down her back that had nothing to do with the wind.

The deeper she walked, the more the trees leaned in. Their trunks grew closer together, their branches tangled overhead like a canopy of knotted fingers. The air felt heavier here. The silence thicker.

Twenty minutes passed in a blur of breath and broken twigs.

Then, just as her patience began to crack, the woods parted—barely—and she saw it.

Cabin 0.

It didn't stand so much as *huddle*, half-swallowed by the earth and blanketed in a thick coat of moss. Its porch sagged like a spine bent with age. The roof had partially caved in on the far corner, but the structure still held. Barely.

No windows. No markings. No number on the frame.

It didn't want to be found.

Sloane stepped onto the porch. The boards groaned, slow and pained. A nail gave beneath her heel with a metallic pop.

She tested the door.

It opened.

No resistance. No lock. Just the sound of wood against warped wood, and a gust of air that smelled of mold, rot, and long-closed spaces.

———

The flashlight's beam cut through dust and darkness.

The cabin was smaller than the others. One room. A bedframe sagging in the corner. A fireplace half-collapsed. The walls were dark with water damage and the creeping rot of neglect.

But even in the decay, it felt watched.

Like something had been waiting.

She stepped forward slowly, scanning.

The light slid across a collapsed chair, a rusted nail pounded into the wall behind it—empty now, though it might've once held a coat. A bootprint in the dust. Old, but human.

She crouched beside the chair.

Above it, scratched deep into the wall with something sharp:

"Don't trust RW."

Below that:

"They turn on their own."

Her breath fogged the air. She hadn't even realized it had grown that cold.

———

Near the back wall, her flashlight caught something odd.

A slight rise in the floorboards. Nothing obvious—just one board, a little darker, a little more rigid than the rest. Newer.

She tapped it. Hollow.

Tried to lift it.

Nothing.

The board didn't budge.

She ran her fingernails along the seam. Still nothing.

It wasn't just stuck.

It didn't want to open.

She reached into her coat pocket, pulled out her house key, and wedged the tip between the planks.

The metal scraped. Bit.

She leaned her weight onto it slowly, steadily. The wood groaned. Splintered.

And then—pop.

The board lifted just enough for her to pry it loose.

She sat back on her heels, heart pounding.

Inside the narrow compartment was a bundle wrapped in thick plastic, stained and softened by time. And beneath it, nestled in the dust like something planted:

A cassette tape.

She reached in carefully and pulled it free.

The label was smudged but legible.

"Cabin 3 / Finch / Red Door"

Her pulse roared in her ears.

The Red Door. The bird. Cabin 3.

She slipped the tape into her bag, her breath catching in her throat.

She glanced back into the hollow.

There was something else.

———

Another marking—on the inner side of the board she'd pried up.

Not carved. Burned.

A Pine Siskin.

But not like the others.

This one was wrong.

One wing was missing entirely, just a black smear. Its beak was open, as if mid-scream. And where its eye should have been—only a hollow gouge.

It wasn't the town's bird.

It was something else wearing its shape.

A warning. Or a confession.

———

Then—a sound.

Outside.

A slow, deliberate crunch of leaves.

Then another.

Sloane's heart seized.

She killed the flashlight.

Darkness swallowed the room.

She crouched behind the bedframe, bag clutched tight to her chest, forcing each breath to stay quiet.

The porch creaked once.

Then again.

And then—nothing.

Not silence. Not wind.

Just absence.

As if the forest had drawn a breath and refused to let it go.

She waited, motionless, muscles aching from stillness.

A long minute passed. Then another.

The porch stayed quiet.

Whoever—or *whatever*—had been there… was gone.

———

When she finally moved again, her legs trembled beneath her.

She slipped from the cabin like a shadow, heart racing with every step.

The woods were darker now. Closer. She didn't look back.

Back at Cabin 17, she locked the door behind her and sat on the floor with her back to the wall, clutching the tape like it might disappear.

Delia had been there.

She'd left a message.

And Sloane had it now.

But she wasn't the only one looking.

Chapter 12
The Voice in the Static

The cassette player sat in the middle of the rug like a relic, small and black and slightly warm from the batteries she'd salvaged from an old flashlight. Everything else in the cabin had gone quiet.

Sloane had turned off the lights.

Only the soft gold from the fireplace flickered across the floor, its flames low and whispering like they didn't want to be overheard.

She sat cross-legged on the floor, the walls close, the silence heavy enough to feel.

Her fingers hovered over the PLAY button.

She pressed it.

Click.

A hiss of static bled from the speakers, rising like breath.

For a few seconds, there was nothing but the quiet sizzle of silence.

Then—

"This is... okay. This is recording. My name is Delia Reese."

Sloane's pulse stumbled.

The voice was younger than she expected—uncertain, but not weak. *Alive.*

"If you're hearing this, it means either I made it out... or I didn't."

Sloane swallowed hard. The room felt colder.

"It's Cabin 3. That's where it started. The Red Door's still there. Painted over, but the seams show through if you know where to look."

Sloane's hand tightened on her knee.

She had *just* wondered where the Red Door was.

"You'll know it when you see it. You can feel it hum when you're close. Like a pulse. A warning."

Sloane's eyes flicked to the player.

No way. No way.

"And if you're wondering whether it's real—it is. It's *real.* You're not imagining it."

The air in the room changed.

Heavier.

Like something unseen had joined her on the floor.

Delia's voice dropped to a near-whisper.

"I've been hearing them. In the walls. In the pipes. Breathing under the boards. It's not just one thing. It's... it's the whole place. Like Pine Hollow was built around a wound, and the cabins are just the scabs."

The fire cracked. Loud. Too loud.

Sloane flinched.

"They come at night. I don't know what they are—not exactly—but they wear the town like a mask."

"And I think one of them is inside the Association."

"RW says I need to stop digging. He's scared. Really scared. But it's not for me. He's afraid they'll find out *he* told me."

"I asked him about the Pine Siskin—why it's on everything. He said it's not a symbol."

"It's a seal. It's meant to hold something in."

Sloane blinked. That exact thought—*Is it a seal?*—had crossed her mind seconds before.

And now Delia was answering.

Her breath quickened.

This wasn't just a recording. It felt... aware.

Delia's voice wavered now. Closer to breaking.

"There's a book. I think it's hidden in Cabin 3. Behind the wall. I can't get to it yet. I need to find the old key—the one with the bird etched on it."

"If you find it before I do… don't open it. Not yet. Not unless you're sure you're alone."

"Not unless you know what you're waking up."

A beat of silence. Longer this time.

Then her voice, softer. Barely a breath:

"I think they already know what I've seen."

"They watch me now. Not just at night."

"I see them in the reflection. In windows. In the glass."

"They don't blink."

The tape crackled—distorted. The sound stuttered like it was unraveling.

Delia's voice returned, fast and shaken.

"They're in the walls. I *hear* them."

A bang.

On the tape.

Sloane recoiled.

Delia screamed.

"I didn't open the door—I swear—please—"

Another bang.

"They're inside—!"

Then static.

Thick, roiling, *angry*.

And beneath it—*something else.*

Not words. A whispering texture. Like language just out of reach.

Sloane leaned forward, breath held.

The whisper swelled.

Then stopped.

A voice—low, male, not Delia's—spoke two clear words:

"She knows."

The tape clicked off.

Silence returned.

But it wasn't the same silence.

It was heavier now.

Charged.

As if the tape had left something behind with her.

Sloane sat frozen in the dark, the fire casting long, restless shadows across the rug.

And then—

Knock.

Three slow, deliberate raps at the door.

She didn't move.

Didn't breathe.

Another knock.

Cabin Zero

Chapter 13
What Knocks

The knock echoed through Cabin 17 like it had come from inside the walls.

Sloane didn't move.

The cassette player sat silent on the rug, its buttons glinting softly in the dying firelight. The air had gone cold, as if the cabin itself had inhaled—and forgotten to exhale.

Three knocks.
Deliberate.
Measured.
Patient.

She rose to her feet slowly, her legs stiff, her breath shallow. The fire behind her popped once—sharp and dry—and cast a wave of warped shadows across the room. One of them stretched too long, too wide.

She ignored it.

Each step toward the front door felt like it took too long. The old boards beneath her bare feet felt unfamiliar. Almost soft.

She paused, hand on the lock.

The last time she'd opened a door like this, it had led to a place that shouldn't have existed.

This one might be worse.

She turned the bolt.

And opened the door.

———

The cold hit her first.

Not wind. Not air. Just stillness.

Outside, the trees stood frozen in place, their black limbs webbing across the sky. The clearing around her cabin was hushed, as if every sound had been scooped out and buried deep.

No person.

No shape in the dark.

But something had been here.

She stepped forward, slowly, her flashlight trembling in her hand.

Then she saw it.

Centered neatly on the welcome mat:

A single feather.

Long and delicate. Soft gray streaked with brown and gold.

A Pine Siskin feather.

Its quill was wrapped in something faintly pink—faded, frayed ribbon, tied with the trembling care of a child wrapping a secret.

Sloane knelt slowly. The air was colder the closer she got to it.

She reached out.

The feather was warm.

Not just from the porch wood—*fresh*. Like someone had placed it there seconds ago.

And beneath it—something else.

A faint bootprint, pressed into the pine needles just off the porch. Smaller than hers. Familiar.

Cabin 0.

The same tread.

She looked up.

The trees were still.

But she felt them watching.

She stepped backward into the cabin, closed the door slowly, then turned the lock.

Then the deadbolt.

The lights flickered overhead—once, twice—and held. The fire behind her had burned to a dull red hum.

She moved down the hallway, quiet, careful.

Her father's room was still. The air smelled like old flannel and sleeping dust.

But Jack wasn't asleep.

He sat on the edge of his bed, hands loose in his lap, staring at the corner of the room.

"Dad?"

No answer.

She stepped closer. The shadows along the baseboard seemed to stretch, curving toward his feet like roots.

"Dad, did you hear—"

Then he spoke.

Low.

Too clear.

"They never cared about the door."

She froze.

Jack turned slowly toward her, and for the first time in days—weeks—his eyes were sharp. Awake.

"It wasn't the door that scared them," he said. "It was what knew how to open it."

Then the light flickered again.

And just like that, his eyes softened. Dimmed.

He looked down at his hands like he didn't know how they'd gotten there.

"Is it morning?" he whispered. "I was dreaming. There were... birds. A thousand of them."

Sloane reached for his hand.

"It's still night," she said.

But she wasn't sure that was true anymore.

———

She returned to the living room and sat in front of the fire, the feather and ribbon resting in her palms.

She untied the knot.

Inside the coiled ribbon was a brass pendant, no bigger than a coin.

A bird in flight. Its wings flared, its beak open in silent song.

A Pine Siskin.

But older. Worn smooth at the edges like it had been touched a thousand times.

She turned it over.

Scratched into the back, in uneven lines:

D.R.

Delia Reese.

Her pendant.

Sloane stared at it, the weight of it pressing into her palm like a question.

This wasn't a clue.

It was a message.

And it had come a very long way to find her.

Chapter 14
The Red Door

Cabin 3 sat at the end of a path that didn't appear on any official map.

The trees along the way leaned closer than they should've, forming a kind of tunnel overhead—dense pine needles muffling every sound. No birds. No wind. Only the rhythmic crunch of her boots over soft, uneven ground.

The air changed as she neared it.

Colder. Denser. Like stepping into a room where someone had just been, and the air hadn't cleared yet.

Cabin 3 wasn't abandoned. That was immediately clear.

The porch had been swept. The windows were intact, the glass smudged only at the corners. The shutters were painted a deep, somber green that looked too fresh for how old the cabin should be. Even the wood siding had been scrubbed clean of moss.

But something about it felt... wrong.

Not untouched.

Preserved.

Sloane stepped onto the porch. The boards groaned beneath her weight—not in protest, but in recognition.

A gust of wind stirred behind her. The trees rustled once, then fell still again.

She placed her hand on the doorknob.

It turned without resistance.

The door opened silently.

———

The interior was too quiet.

Not just because it was empty—because it was waiting.

Sunlight filtered in through the front windows, pale and angled, casting long rectangles across the polished floor. There was no dust in the air. No scent of decay. Only the faintest trace of something medicinal— like old antiseptic and dried lavender.

The room was neat.

Pristine.

A rug lay centered beneath a small round table, untouched. A single armchair sat in the corner, angled just so. The fireplace was empty but freshly swept, as though someone had cleaned it and then never returned.

Everything was too… arranged.

Like a set.

She stepped further inside, flashlight at her side though she didn't yet need it. Her boots made soft thuds against the floor, the only sound in the house.

She passed a hallway on the left, a darkened bathroom to the right, and turned the corner into what should have been a bedroom.

But it wasn't.

Instead, tucked behind a partially slid bookshelf at the back of the room, was a door.

Painted a deep, chalky red.

Not bright. Not modern.

Blood-dark.

It pulsed faintly in the filtered light. Not movement—just the illusion of breath. The paint was old, cracked slightly along the edges, but it hadn't flaked. It looked… freshly ancient. Sealed and sacred.

Sloane stepped closer, and the temperature shifted again—warmth now. A subtle heat radiated from the door like a fevered body.

She reached out.

Paused.

Pressed her palm flat to its surface.

The wood was warm.

And it hummed.

Low. Vibrational. Like the sound a bone makes when it resonates with something too deep to name.

She staggered back, shaking her hand as if it had burned her.

To the left of the door, the wall paneling changed. Barely. A seam just out of line. Like something had been fitted over it, quickly but not perfectly.

Sloane set her bag down, pulled out her house key, and wedged it into the gap. She pushed, twisted—until the panel gave with a soft snap and folded away like a secret drawer.

Inside: a narrow, hollow space.

A bundle of old, scorched pages, the edges blackened and curled. A fragment of a map, folded once, yellowed and torn at the crease.

She sat cross-legged on the floor, the hum of the Red Door behind her like a second heartbeat.

She unfolded the journal pages.

Delia's handwriting.

Shaky. Quick. Desperate.

"Cabin 3 was the anchor. They built it to hold the pressure, but the structure's failing. It bleeds now. The door breathes."

"I found the sigils beneath the floor. They're not just marks— they're locks. And one's been broken. Cracked near the corner."

Sloane turned to the map—an original site layout of the early cabins. Cabin 3 was circled. But beneath it, someone had drawn faint markings—like roots spidering out from the foundation.

One of the marks was crossed out.

———

She rose, heart pounding, and moved to the fireplace. Shifted the rug.

The floorboards beneath looked slightly newer. Sanded recently. Nails darker than the rest.

She tapped.

Hollow.

She dropped to her knees, pried at the seam.

It didn't want to open.

She pressed harder. Wedged the poker from the fireplace into the gap. The metal bit into the wood with a groan, and the board snapped upward with a crack of protest.

A rush of cold air spilled out.

And something else.

The scent of pine and… iron.

She lowered the flashlight into the dark.

A crawlspace. Tight. Narrow.

Inside, centered beneath the open floor: a bundle of twigs and branches, bound tightly in dark red twine. Shaped like a bird in mid-flight.

A Pine Siskin.

Its wing snapped unnaturally to one side. Its head cocked in warning.

The floor beneath the effigy had been carved.

Symbols radiated outward like a sunburst.

The circle.
The bird.
The seal.

But something was wrong.

The eye was gone.

Gouged out.

Burned black.

A warning.

Not from Delia.

From the cabin.

———

Then —

A sound behind her.

From the Red Door.

One knock.

Then another.

Then silence.

But not stillness.

She turned, flashlight shaking slightly in her hand, and stepped back from the open floor.

The door didn't open.

Didn't move.

But it breathed.

And behind it—*something waited.*

Chapter 15
The Threshold

The Red Door loomed like a secret holding its breath.

It didn't rattle. Didn't whisper. It simply stood—*still,* too still—in the back wall of Cabin 3. Its deep, rusted crimson soaked up the sunlight like old blood. Not a hint of shine. Just weight, like the color had been painted in grief.

Sloane stood inches from it, every hair on her arms lifting with something that felt less like fear and more like recognition.

The door wasn't resisting.

It was waiting.

She reached out, pressed her hand flat to its center.

Warm.

But not like sun-warmed wood. This was body-warmth. Like touching someone's chest. Like pulse beneath flesh. And beneath her palm, she felt it—

A soft vibration.

A hum.

Low and steady. Not mechanical. Not alive.

Something else.

Her breath clouded slightly in the air, though the cabin wasn't cold. Her voice came out quieter than intended, carried by the hush that filled the space:

"Every door needs someone to open it."

And maybe this one had been waiting for her.

She pressed.

The wood gave.

Just a fraction—but enough.

A soft, groaning shift echoed down through the frame, like the cabin itself had exhaled.

With a slow, careful push, Sloane opened the Red Door.

———

A sharp breath of air met her, cold and clean, but not in a way that brought relief. It smelled of damp stone and earth long undisturbed. A sterile kind of rot. Like the inside of a sealed crypt.

Her flashlight beam cut into the dark beyond the door.

A corridor, narrow and steep, descended in slick stone steps. The walls were rough-hewn, the air tight. Drops of condensation clung to the ceiling like sweat.

She hesitated only a moment before stepping through.

The door whispered shut behind her, and the darkness swallowed the sound whole.

———

Each step down felt older than the last.

The stone beneath her boots was worn smooth—not recently, but over time. Centuries, maybe. The walls curved in slightly, forcing her shoulders inward. Water beaded along seams in the mortar, tracing paths like veins. The silence pressed in, thick as velvet.

Sconces lined the corridor—ancient iron fixtures sunk into the rock, their candle wax long gone. A few held only blackened stumps, melted to the bone. The metal was cold as she brushed it in passing. The dust was… absent.

Like someone had come through not long ago.

Or like nothing settled here. Not even time.

At the end of the corridor, the passage opened.

A room, no bigger than a root cellar, square-cut from the stone. The temperature dropped instantly.

Her light swept across bare walls, then caught on something in the center.

A chair.

Wooden. Narrow. Hand-carved. Positioned exactly in the center of a circular engraving etched into the floor.

She stepped closer, slowly, beam steady.

The engraving was familiar.

A Pine Siskin.

Wings flared in full spread. Talons extended. Its eye open wide.

But the beak

Was gone.

Not broken.

Never carved.

Just a smooth space where the mouth should be.

A bird that could watch.

But never speak.

———

On the far wall, gouges.

Scratches clawed into the stone, uneven and furious. Words layered over themselves in long vertical lines:

SPEAK
SPEAK
SPEAK
SPEAK—

Dozens. Maybe hundreds.

Each one more erratic than the last.

The wall beneath the final lines had crumbled, like something had slammed against it from the inside.

Sloane's throat tightened.

The silence in this place wasn't empty. It was crowded.

She turned back to the chair.

The circle beneath it was cracked. Hairline fractures radiated out like splintered glass beneath ice. One of the grooves in the carving was darker than the rest. Burned.

A smell drifted up from it—sharp. Metallic. Like iron and old breath.

She crouched, slowly, and ran her hand along the groove.

It was warm.

Beneath The Pines

Then—

A shift behind her.

Soft. Deliberate.

The flashlight beam jumped as she turned.

Nothing.

Just shadows clinging to the uneven walls like they belonged there.

And yet...

Her skin prickled.

The hair at the nape of her neck lifted.

She wasn't alone.

Not in a "someone just entered" kind of way.

In a "someone never left" kind of way.

The air behind her moved.

A whisper.

Not a voice.

Not a word.

Just a breath—

So close she could feel it graze the back of her neck.

Then a voice, low and intimate, just behind her ear:

"Thank you."

Her heart seized.

She turned sharply, flashlight swinging through the air.

The beam flickered—once, twice—before holding.

The room was the same.

The door behind her still open.

No figure.

No breath.

No shadow out of place.

But the chair—

Was no longer facing the circle.

It was facing her.

Chapter 16
What Lies Beneath

The chair didn't creak.

It didn't scrape or shift or groan. It simply was—now facing her, when a moment before it hadn't been.

And that was worse than any noise.

Sloane froze.

The carved wooden legs were rooted to the center of the floor, anchored in the same place as before—only now perfectly aligned with the open Red Door behind her. It hadn't moved. There was no drag mark on the stone. No sound of turning.

Just the chair. Watching her. Inviting her.

She could hear her own breath—too loud, too fast. The rest of the chamber was silent, but not still. It vibrated in her bones like the moment before a building groans in an earthquake. The hum that never reaches the ears, only the chest.

Her flashlight wavered slightly in her hand.

The air had thickened—saturated with cold, heavy with something more than dampness. The scent of moss and earth had given way to something metallic and dark, like wet iron and wilted roses. Faint. Beautiful. Wrong.

She stepped forward.

The beam of her flashlight carved through the stillness, slicing across stone walls that glistened faintly with condensation. The moisture ran in tiny rivulets, tracing the seams of the ancient blocks like veins. The stone looked older down here than anything above it—rough, porous, like it had been dug out by hand and never meant to be found again.

The chair waited in the center of a shallow depression in the floor. Around it, carved deeply into the stone, was a symbol she now knew intimately:

The Pine Siskin.

But not the clean, proud image used on town signage.

This one was older. Raw.

Its wings were wide, feathers stretched to sharp points. Its eye was open, rimmed in uneven lines as if someone had circled it over and over in fear.

But its beak—

Was missing.

Not broken. Not unfinished.

Smoothed away, as if erased. Like someone had tried to silence it.

A bird that could only watch.

Never speak.

———

She moved closer, slowly, her boots scuffing against the etched circle.

The chair was hand-carved. Narrow. High-backed. Its grain was dark and rippled, smoothed in places from use—or from touch. As her beam passed over the upper rail, she noticed something faint: a line of initials carved so lightly they nearly disappeared into the wood.

D.R.

Delia.

Sloane reached out and let her fingertips graze the armrest.

Warm.

Too warm for a chair that should've sat in cold silence for years.

It felt like someone had just left it.

She turned slowly, scanning the floor again. Beyond the circle, near the edge of the chamber, her light caught the glint of iron—a small grate, nearly flush with the stone. Rust had darkened its edges, and moisture beaded along the cracks.

She knelt. Shined the light through the bars.

Below: darkness.

Stone and dirt. The faint outline of space beneath. And something else—

Movement.

A flicker, low and slow. Just enough to make her pull the light back and hold her breath.

Then the sound began.

At first, she thought it was dripping.

But it was too steady.

Scratch.

Scratch.

Pause.

Scratch.

Rhythmic. Deliberate.

Like nails. Like claws.

On stone.

Coming from beneath the floor.

———

She stood abruptly, stepping away from the grate, every part of her on edge.

The light caught on something new.

The wall behind the chair—where the old gouges read *SPEAK* over and over—had changed.

Lower down, where dust and time should have blanketed the surface, the stone was freshly marked. Still sharp.

STAY

Etched with precision. Recent.

Sloane stared at it, and her flashlight began to flicker again. Just for a moment. But long enough to make her shadow jump—long enough to remind her she was not alone.

She turned back to the corridor she came from. The narrow hallway that had led her into this chamber was still there, still open.

But it looked… farther now.

As if the distance between her and the exit had stretched without moving.

As if the door wanted her to feel it.

She stepped back toward the tunnel, toward the dim sliver of the cabin beyond.

The chair didn't move again.

But she could still feel it watching her.

She passed the Red Door, still open behind her, the same muted crimson catching what little light her flashlight offered. As she reached the threshold, she paused.

One last look.

The circle. The carving. The grate.
The chair.

Whatever this room was… it wasn't just buried.

It was kept.

And someone—or something—had been waiting.

She stepped through the doorway.

And the moment her foot hit the wood floor of the cabin—

SLAM.

The Red Door snapped shut behind her with the sound of finality, like a judge's gavel or a tomb being sealed.

She spun, breath caught in her chest.

The door was gone.

Where it had been just seconds before was now smooth wall paneling. Seamless. Clean. Not a single trace of paint. No handle. No hinges. No outline.

As if it had never existed.

As if she had imagined it.

Except her hands still smelled of stone and rust and old air.

She stepped backward, slowly, heart thudding.

The cabin creaked once—softly. Not settling.

Responding.

Chapter 17
The Ones Who Remember

Sloane didn't sleep that night.

She tried. She lay in the dark with the covers pulled tight beneath her chin, the ceiling above her no longer just wood and beams but something aware—like it was listening for her breath. The cabin creaked softly, but not from settling. The sounds were too measured. Too spaced. Like footsteps… taken slowly… around the edges of her consciousness.

She had washed her hands twice after returning from Cabin 3.

Scrubbed them until they were pink, the scent of rust and stone rinsing into the sink like it could be erased.

It lingered anyway.

Like something buried under her skin.

By two a.m., she had turned every light on.

By four, she had turned them all off again.

When the sun finally started to rise—thin and sickly, barely more than a gray smear above the trees—Sloane was still awake, sitting in the armchair near the front window, watching the mist curl along the cabin porches like smoke from a slow, cold fire.

Outside, the gravel path glistened from rain that must've fallen in the early hours. The forest steamed. The trees didn't sway. They stood still, as if the storm had left them stunned.

As if they knew.

————

Her phone buzzed once.

No signal.

But a voicemail alert blinked on the screen.

No number. No timestamp. Just the word: *Message.*

She hesitated.

Then pressed play.

The speaker hissed softly.

At first, just wind. Sharp, high, whipping through something narrow—branches, maybe.

Then a voice. Not Delia's. Not Jack's. Not hers.

Soft.

Uncertain.

"She saw."

Click.

The line cut.

The room fell so silent afterward she could hear the blood in her ears.

————

She dressed in silence. Jeans, boots, sweater. She tied her hair back like her hands needed something to do. Her reflection in the bathroom mirror looked thinner somehow—like whatever had happened beneath the Red Door had stripped something away.

Outside, the mist hung low and heavy, casting the cabins in soft gray outlines. Everything was muted—the sky, the ground, even her own thoughts.

She walked toward town with the pendant still tucked in her pocket.

The one with Delia's initials.

The bakery bell jangled as she stepped inside.

Warmth hit her like a wave, too thick, too sweet—yeast, sugar, cinnamon—but it felt artificial now. Like it was trying too hard to hide something burning underneath.

Birdie stood behind the counter, hair pinned back, hands dusted with flour. She looked up as Sloane entered.

And paused.

Just for a heartbeat.

Her smile came a second late.

"Sugar," she said, her southern drawl laid on like syrup over sour fruit, "you look like you saw a ghost."

Sloane stepped up to the counter. "Did I?"

Birdie didn't blink. "Why don't you tell me?"

"I went to Cabin 3."

The smile faltered—just a flicker, just around the eyes.

"I found the Red Door," Sloane said.

Birdie didn't move.

"Did you know what was beneath it?"

Silence.

Then the soft clink of a ceramic mug being placed on the counter.

"Coffee?" Birdie asked, tone returning to polite.

Sloane took it.

"You ever seen the room beneath it?"

Birdie turned to pour.

"I try not to talk about things that don't exist," she said quietly. "That's how we keep the peace."

Sloane leaned in. "Peace doesn't feel like the right word."

Birdie's eyes stayed on the pot as it filled. She placed the cup between them and looked up.

"It's not the Red Door we feared," she said. "It's the ones who walk back out of it."

———

Back at Cabin 17, the air inside felt stale. Like it had been holding its breath while she was gone.

She closed the door behind her and turned to find her father standing in the hallway.

Not seated.

Standing.

His hand was pressed flat against the wall, as if listening through it.

His back was too straight. His shoulders too rigid. Like something else was propping him up.

"Dad?"

He didn't turn.

Sloane approached slowly.

When he did face her, his eyes were too wide. Too bright.

"I felt her," he whispered.

"Who?"

His lips barely moved.

"The girl. The one who never came home."

———

That night, Sloane stripped the bed and remade it with fresh sheets. She turned every lamp off except one. The fire in the hearth crackled low, steady, but couldn't quite chase away the chill that had taken root in the walls.

She slid her notebook from her bag and flipped to a clean page.

At the top, she wrote:

> *Cabin 3 opened.*
> *Red Door real.*
> *Not alone.*

She stopped when she reached the word *opened.*

The page felt too thin to hold what had happened.

She folded the notebook closed.

———

It wasn't until she turned back the bed covers that she saw it.

Something tucked beneath her pillow.

Not a note.

A page.

Torn. Edges scorched. Ink smudged.

But still legible.

Delia's handwriting.

*"I thought the cabins were built to protect us.
But they were built to contain something else."*

At the bottom of the page, a familiar symbol had been drawn in the corner:

The Pine Siskin.

But this one had an open beak.

Screaming.

And the circle around it?

Broken.

Split clean down the middle like something had shattered it from within.

Chapter 18
What We Bury

The knock came just after sundown.

Not sharp. Not urgent.

Three dull raps against the screen door—uneven, soft, like someone wasn't sure if they wanted to be answered.

Sloane crossed the room slowly, tension already coiling in her shoulders. The fire crackled behind her, low and steady, but the rest of the cabin had fallen silent. The kind of silence that listened.

She opened the door.

And found a man standing on her porch.

He looked like he belonged to the town—but not in the clean, smiling way people like Birdie or Caleb did.

This man belonged to the bones of Pine Hollow.

He was tall and sun-worn, early thirties maybe, with a lean frame that looked like it had spent a lifetime carrying too much. His work shirt was faded nearly to gray, buttons mismatched, sleeves rolled just below the elbow. Boots caked in mud. Toolbelt hanging low, slouched from use.

His jaw was shadowed in stubble, and his eyes—dark and rimmed with sleeplessness—studied her like a man looking for permission.

"Miss Wren?" he asked.

His voice was gravel. Unsmoked for a while, but rough all the same.

She didn't reply.

He shifted his weight. Didn't move closer. Just… waited.

"I'm not here to cause any trouble," he said. "Name's Cal Mercer."

Sloane's stomach tightened at the name.

Mercer.

One of the old names.

Founders. Association royalty.

"You're related to Nora Mercer?"

He looked away.

"She's my mother," he said. "Though she wouldn't admit that out loud anymore."

His mouth curled into something bitter that might've once been a smile.

"I work grounds for the Preservation Society. Cabins. Trail paths. Plumbing when it leaks, gas lines when they hum. They don't put my name on anything. But I've been under every cabin in this place."

Still, Sloane didn't speak.

"I heard you opened it," he said. "Cabin 3. The Red Door."

Her hand tightened on the edge of the doorframe.

"I didn't tell anyone."

"I know," he said. "But I felt it."

She stepped aside.

He walked in like a man who didn't expect warmth, who had learned to live in doorways and crawlspaces and silence.

———

He didn't sit.

He stood in the middle of the room, back to the fire, eyes scanning the walls like they might speak before he did.

"I was thirteen," he said after a while. "The first time my father took me under one of the cabins. Number 48, I think. Summer had just broken and the crawlspace was dry. Hot. Smelled like dust and copper."

Sloane leaned against the counter.

"We weren't there to fix anything," he continued. "He handed me a bag. Heavy. Told me not to open it. Just dig. We were putting it down. Sealing it."

He looked at her now.

"I asked what it was."

"And?"

"He told me to shut up."

Cal's voice cracked, just barely.

"I still remember the sound it made when we dropped it into the hole. Like… it hit something soft underneath."

He swallowed hard. Looked down at his hands like they weren't his.

"After that, the dreams started."

Sloane stayed quiet. Let him speak.

"I couldn't sleep. Couldn't concentrate. Every night I'd wake up to that same sound—over and over. That *thud*. And whispers… but not in words. Just pressure. Like something crawling behind the walls, trying to remember how to speak."

He ran a hand through his hair. The motion trembled.

"I started using when I was seventeen. First pills. Then whatever I could get. I just needed it to stop." He paused. "My mom—Nora—cut me off. She told people I left town. They locked me out of the family name."

"How long were you out?"

"Six years. I came back after my dad died. They said heart attack. But he was in Cabin 3 the week before it happened. Alone."

He stepped closer to the fire.

"I sobered up two years ago. I fix what they let me fix. I keep quiet. It's the deal."

"Until now," Sloane said.

He nodded.

"Because when you opened that door?" he whispered. "I felt it snap. Like a rubber band stretched too long finally breaking. Something gave way."

He reached into the inner pocket of his coat and pulled out a folded map.

She took it gently, unfolding it across the coffee table. Her breath caught.

It wasn't a plat map.

It was a cross-section—of Pine Hollow.

From beneath.

Lines spidered out under the cabins. Crawlspaces. Drainage channels. Forgotten utility routes. And symbols—some she recognized from the Preservation Society's archived maps, others drawn by hand.

Circles.

Marks.

Birds.

Seals.

One with a jagged red slash through it—Cabin 3.

At the base of the map, near the bottom right corner, something was labeled in a shaky, penciled scrawl:

THE ROOT.

"They built the town around it," Cal said quietly. "Tried to pin it down. Anchor it."

"And now?"

Cal looked at her.

Tired. Worn. But clear.

"Now it's pulling back."

Sloane traced one line with her finger.

It ran directly beneath Cabin 17.

She looked up.

"You think I caused this."

"No," he said. "I think you're the reason it hasn't gotten worse."

She blinked.

"I think… it's been waiting for someone to come back in." He paused. "Someone who could walk out without forgetting."

Sloane let that settle in the silence.

Then:

"Why me?"

Cal hesitated.

Then leaned forward.

"Because you don't scare easy," he said. "And you opened the door. Every door needs someone to open it, right?"

She stared at the map again.

And the Root waited beneath it all.

Chapter 19
Beneath the Silence

Cabin Zero looked smaller the second time.

Not just physically—but as if the woods had grown around it. Swallowed it. The trees that ringed its clearing now leaned inward like watchful sentries, their branches knitting overhead to form a jagged crown of pine.

The roof sagged deeper. The moss had thickened. The air around it felt heavier than before—humid and still, like the breath of a sleeper who hasn't stirred in too long.

Sloane stood at the edge of the clearing with Cal beside her, both of them silent.

The quiet here was different.

It wasn't just an absence of sound.

It was a presence.

A pressure in the air.

A weight on the bones.

A silence with memory.

Sloane stepped forward.

The porch groaned beneath her boot like it recognized her.

The front door gave on the first try, hinges releasing with a reluctant creak.

And they stepped into the dark.

———

The smell had changed.

The first time, it had been mold and dust. Old cabin decay. Familiar, if a little sour.

Now it smelled like deep earth—wet roots, iron, something like spoiled flowers. Like rot… dressed up for a funeral.

Cal lingered just inside the door, eyes sweeping the cabin's interior.

He looked more alert than before. Not nervous. Not afraid.

Haunted.

"I've been under every cabin," he said quietly. "Every crawlspace. Every drain line. But not this one. They told me it didn't exist."

Sloane nodded toward the back wall. "I found a compartment under the bed. That's where Delia left the tape."

He crossed the room and crouched beside the bedframe, running his hand along the baseboard.

"See this?" he said. "That nail. It's new. Someone's been here since you came."

"Someone trying to hide it again."

"Or trying to keep it sealed."

His voice dropped as he said it, as if speaking too loudly might wake something.

———

They moved through the room slowly, searching, until Cal stopped near the back wall. His palm slid along the floor, pausing where the wood grain shifted.

"Here."

Sloane knelt beside him.

There—just above the baseboard—was a faint seam. Barely visible. A panel cut into the wall and almost perfectly disguised.

Cal pulled a multitool from his belt and wedged the blade beneath the seam. Sloane braced the edge with her key.

The panel resisted at first—stiff, swollen with time and damp.

Then it popped, swinging inward with a soft exhale of dust and cold.

Behind it was darkness.

And a tunnel.

The entrance was barely four feet tall and only wide enough for a body to crawl through.

The stone was slick. Blackened. The earth pressed in from both sides like the ribs of something ancient and hollowed out.

They exchanged a look.

Cal clicked on his flashlight. The beam pierced the dark ahead.

He nodded once.

Then dropped to his knees and crawled inside.

Sloane followed, the light from the cabin swallowed almost instantly behind them.

The tunnel dropped them into silence.

Not quiet.

True silence.

Like sound had been scraped out of the air.

Their movements felt louder than they should have—knees scuffing against stone, breath echoing back too fast. Water dripped somewhere ahead, slow and steady, like the ticking of a clock wound too tightly.

Roots hung from the ceiling like strands of old rope. Some pulsed faintly. Others seemed to twitch just out of sight.

The deeper they went, the closer the air got.

Not colder. Just closer—thicker, like breathing in a room with no windows.

Then the tunnel opened.

And they stepped into a chamber.

———

It was small, no wider than a toolshed. The walls were carved stone, but smoother here—intentional. Symbols lined the edges, faded by time and damp.

And at the far end, a door.

Iron. Riveted.

Twice as tall as the tunnel they'd just crawled through, and wide enough for something larger than a person to pass.

It had no handle. No latch.

Just a single metal plate bolted at its center.

On it was the Pine Siskin.

But it was wrong.

The wings were barbed. The feathers sharp like blades. Its eye was carved deeper than necessary, almost gouged.

And its beak—once sealed shut on every symbol they'd seen—

Was now open.

Screaming in silence.

———

Cal stared at it, frozen.

"I know this," he whispered.

Sloane turned to him.

"I've never seen it before. Not really. But I've dreamed it. For years. I thought it was the drugs. But it was this."

She stepped closer to the door.

Engraved just beneath the screaming bird, the metal had oxidized around a line of text, barely legible through the rust:

"Beneath silence, it listens."
"Beneath listening, it waits."

She reached out.

Didn't touch it.

Just hovered her fingers above the plate.

She could feel it vibrating—faintly. Like a heartbeat trapped in steel.

Cal backed up a step.

"We shouldn't have come here."

Sloane lowered her hand.

"We didn't come here."

She turned to him.

"We were called."

———

Then the lights died.

Both flashlights cut out in the same instant—snuffed like candles in a cold wind.

The darkness closed around them.

Total.

Complete.

Something moved in it.

Not fast.

Not loud.

Just present.

And beneath their feet, the stone began to warm.

Like something was waking up beneath it.

Chapter 20
The Cracking Ground

The power came back thirty seconds after it died.

But nothing felt the same.

Sloane's flashlight sputtered first—its beam twitching, then steadying with a soft electrical pop. It sliced through the dense dark of the chamber, catching Cal's face in a strobe of white.

His eyes were wide.

Still, neither of them spoke.

Because in those thirty seconds of darkness, the room had felt… occupied.

The air hadn't just been cold—it had moved

Whispered.

Not with sound, but with intention.

Now, it was still again.

Too still.

Sloane's gaze dropped to the floor beneath her boots. The stone that had once been dry and dead now pulsed faintly with warmth—slow and rhythmic, like the throb of distant machinery buried deep underground. The engraved symbols glistened, beads of condensation forming along their edges as if the stone itself were sweating.

And in the center of the iron door, the screaming Pine Siskin—its eye seemed deeper than before.

Or maybe it had always been that deep, and now… she could finally see into it.

"We need to go," Cal said softly.

His voice wasn't afraid.

It was resigned.

Like someone who had waited years to be proven right.

Sloane nodded.

Not because she agreed—

Because something in her chest had started to ache with wanting.

A pull.

Like the door was calling her by name.

———

They crawled back through the tunnel in silence.

The space felt tighter now. The roots that dripped from the ceiling twitched slightly in the edge of their flashlights, slick with a syrupy black moisture that clung to her sleeves. Somewhere behind them, water dripped at a steady rhythm—drip… drip… drip—but the sound was no longer benign.

It was counting.

They emerged into Cabin Zero as the last thread of daylight collapsed into dusk.

But the light outside wasn't right.

————

The sky had turned the color of dying embers.

A deep, swollen red bled through the clouds, staining the treetops in a bruised, unnatural glow. It painted the cabins with long, blood-colored shadows that twisted with every flicker of wind.

The air outside was sharp with scent—burnt copper and scorched pine—like the after-smell of a struck match left too long against the skin.

And beneath it all: smoke.

Not thick. Not choking.

Just enough to bite the back of the throat.

Cal stood beside her on the porch of Cabin Zero, staring up at the sky with the hollow stillness of someone seeing a bad dream return.

"I've smelled that before," he murmured. "Only once. When I was a kid. After my dad took me under Cabin 48."

"What does it mean?"

He didn't answer.

He just stepped off the porch and started walking.

————

Back at Cabin 17, the lights were out.

No power. No firelight.

Just the red glow from the forest pressing through the windows like a warning.

Sloane opened the door slowly, heart already tightening.

Her father was standing again.

But not in his usual place.

Not at the wall.

Not in the hallway.

He was at the window.

Still as a cutout. Hands at his sides. Shoulders squared like a soldier.

"Dad?"

He didn't move.

Sloane crossed the room, careful not to break whatever spell held him there.

When she reached his side, she looked into his face—

And stopped.

His eyes were clear.

Focused.

Sharp in a way she hadn't seen since she arrived.

He was watching the trees.

Not blankly.

Studying them.

"Dad, what are you looking at?"

His lips moved. No sound at first.

Then—

He lifted a hand, slowly, and pointed.

"There," he whispered. "Between the trees."

Sloane turned.

And saw it.

A figure.

Motionless. Half-swallowed by shadow, but there. Tall. Still. Watching the cabin.

She blinked—and it was gone.

Her father's voice cracked beside her.

"They've started waking the old ones."

She turned back to him. His face had shifted again—softening, breaking.

"The ones we locked away," he said, voice brittle. "The ones that never really slept."

She stared.

"You knew?"

"I helped."

And then he began to cry.

———

She stayed up the rest of the night.

Across the table, Cal sat hunched over the map, eyes ringed in shadow. A mug of untouched coffee cooled beside him. His hands shook as he traced a finger along the lines.

"You see this curve?"

Sloane leaned closer.

It wasn't a pipe.

It was a spiral.

Not tight like a coil—wide, sweeping through the underside of the cabins like a slow whirlpool drawn in ink.

At the center of the spiral: no cabin number.

Just a symbol.

THE ROOT.

Sloane whispered it aloud.

Cal looked up at her.

His voice was quieter than she'd ever heard it.

"I think Cabin Zero was never meant to hold anything."

He swallowed hard.

"I think it was meant to distract us from what actually needs keeping down."

Sloane stared at the map.

At the spiral.

At the Root.

"And you think it's growing?"

"I think…" Cal paused, eyes flicking toward the dark window. "I think it's hungry."

Chapter 21
The Architect

Morning in Pine Hollow arrived like a held breath.

The fog didn't lift with the sun—it coiled, low and thick, like a living thing curling through the trees. It slid beneath porch rails, wrapped around cabin foundations, and drifted in tendrils across gravel paths like it was searching.

Sloane stood on the back steps of Cabin 17, sipping cold coffee and watching the mist crawl toward the tree line. The air carried the smell of damp bark and unsettled earth—like the ground itself had shifted in its sleep.

Behind her, Cal hovered at the window, jaw tense.

Neither of them had spoken much since the night before.

Since the door.

Since her father's words.

Since the map had drawn a spiral beneath everything.

Now that spiral had a name: The Root.

"I know someone," Cal said quietly. "Who might still know more."

Sloane turned.

He didn't look at her when he added, "My mother."

———

Nora Mercer's house sat on the far edge of town like it didn't belong to Pine Hollow at all.

Set behind a black iron gate and a perfectly trimmed boxwood hedge, the two-story Colonial loomed pale and precise beneath the moss-draped oaks. Every shutter was painted the same shade of deep hunter green. The brass door knocker gleamed. The porch was swept bare.

It was the kind of house that looked empty, even when someone was home.

The kind that knew how to keep secrets in the walls.

Cal hesitated at the gate.

"She hasn't spoken to me since the hospital," he said. "Not in words that weren't warnings."

Sloane nodded once.

They didn't knock.

Because the door opened before they reached it.

———

Nora Mercer stood in the entryway, backlit by gold-toned light, her hand resting gently on the frame like a woman greeting guests to a funeral reception.

She was tall, composed, and severe in a way that didn't require sharpness. Her power came from stillness. Hair pulled into a French twist without a single strand out of place. A deep slate-gray blazer, tailored like armor. No jewelry except a thin silver band on her left hand.

Her eyes landed on Sloane first.

Not Cal.

And she said, simply:

"You've made a mess."

Her voice was smooth. Mid-Atlantic and measured. A voice honed at country club luncheons and boardroom votes.

She stepped back to let them in, without invitation or warmth.

The door clicked shut behind them like a judgment.

———

The interior was immaculate.

Too immaculate.

Not just clean—curated. Cold. Glossed in muted neutrals and fine finishes. The scent of polished wood and dried lavender clung faintly to the air, layered over a deeper, aged note that smelled like dust sealed into antique books.

Sloane's eyes moved across the framed maps lining the hall: vintage plat drawings of Pine Hollow, land surveys with tight cursive notations, old cabin placements.

None of them showed Cabin Zero.
None showed the spiral.

But one—faintly stained by time—featured the original seal.

The Pine Siskin.

Its wings outstretched in perfect symmetry. Beak closed. Tail feather touching a fine circle.

Except this one had a thin crack running through the middle.

Hairline.

Intentional.

She didn't speak.

Nora led them to a sitting room dressed in pale gray and ivory. A tea service waited on a silver tray. She poured with the grace of a woman who'd practiced the motion her entire life.

And said, "We didn't build Pine Hollow to be beautiful."

———

Sloane took the cup. Didn't drink.

Nora sat across from her, hands folded like a portrait come to life.

"We built it to hold."

"Hold what?" Sloane asked.

Nora's lips barely moved. "You've already met it."

Cal hadn't sat.

He stood near the window, arms crossed, spine too stiff.

"You never told me," he said.

Nora didn't look at him.

"I told you to stay away," she said. "You were never meant to carry this."

"I wasn't supposed to survive it, you mean."

That earned her gaze.

It was cool. Measured.

But for a second, something flickered beneath it. Regret, maybe. Or disappointment.

Sloane leaned in slightly.

"My father knew," she said. "Didn't he?"

Nora's eyes softened a degree.

"Jack Wren had the heart of a good man," she said. "But he had the curse of a curious one. He asked questions he shouldn't have. Then he stopped asking. For your sake."

She picked up her tea.

Sipped once.

"It's better to forget some things. That's why the Association exists."

"To keep people safe?" Sloane asked.

"To keep the town intact."

———

Cal stepped forward then, voice shaking but low.

"I overdosed alone behind Cabin 48. You knew what they'd buried under it."

She looked at him for a long, silent moment.

Then said:

"I knew what they'd buried under all of it."

The words landed hard.

And then softly—like a knife slipped between ribs.

"You were never supposed to see it, Cal. You were supposed to leave this town. Not live under it."

He looked at the floor.

Bitter.

Broken.

Sloane sat back.

"The Root is real," she said. "The spiral's not a metaphor. And something's moving."

Nora's expression didn't shift.

"It never stopped moving."

"Then why seal it?"

Nora tilted her head.

"Because belief is fragile. Because the seal gave the town permission to pretend."

She stood.

Walked to the window.

"But pretending doesn't hold forever. Not against something that remembers."

She turned to face them again.

"You didn't just open a door, Miss Wren."
"You woke something that knows your name."

Chapter 22
The Spiral Path

They left before the sun rose.

The sky was still black when they crossed the gravel path behind Cabin 17, and the trees stood like columns of ink, unmoving in the windless dark. Fog clung to the forest floor in low, rolling sheets, weaving between trunks, rising and falling like breath held too long.

Cal walked ahead, his boots muffled by wet moss and layered pine needles. A flashlight clipped to his chest lit the way in narrow bursts—sharp-edged cones of white that sliced through the fog like scalpels through gauze.

He didn't speak.

Neither did Sloane.

Not yet.

The deeper they moved into the woods, the more the trees began to bend—not just in shape, but in alignment.

They curved ever so slightly toward the left, trunks tilting like bodies leaning toward something distant and central. Branches arched overhead in a way that blocked out the sky completely, forming a loose spiral of tangled limbs.

The path itself was barely a path. More suggestion than structure.

The forest floor grew soft beneath her boots. Not muddy. Not earthy.

Pliable.

It gave under her steps like something remembering how to resist.

The smell shifted, too.

Gone was the sharp bite of pine and cold dew. It was replaced by something darker—wet stone, iron, root-rot, and the faintest trace of something sweet and rancid, like flowers long past bloom.

"Do you feel that?" she asked.

Cal's voice was quiet. "It starts here."

———

They passed the first marker ten minutes in.

At the base of a massive black pine, nearly lost to shadow, the bark had been branded with a symbol.

The Pine Siskin.

Its wings outstretched. Beak wide open.

But its eye had been gouged out—burned, not carved. Charred lines spidered out from the hollow like veins feeding into a deeper wound.

"First turn of the spiral," Cal said.

"They marked it?"

"No. They tried to unmark it. Burn it away. But the symbols always grow back."

Sloane knelt beside the tree.

The wood around the symbol was warm. Not from sun. There hadn't been sun.

From within.

She stood quickly and kept moving.

As they walked, the spiral pulled tighter.

The trees crowded closer. The roots grew thicker, rising above the ground in coils and arcs like petrified serpents. Some were slick. Others split open at the tips, revealing pale centers threaded with black.

At one point, she stepped between two narrow trunks and felt her breath catch in her chest—

The air inside that arch was colder.

And her ears popped, like pressure had shifted.

"You passed through it," Cal said from behind her.

"What?"

"The ring. Every spiral has one. Once you cross it, things change."

The trees began to whisper.

Not with wind—there wasn't any.

But with soundless motion, like something brushing the branches just beyond her line of sight. Shapes flickered through the mist. Never fully seen. Never fully gone.

"Keep your eyes ahead," Cal said.

He didn't look around.

Sloane kept walking.

The forest floor glistened now—dark with moisture, patterned in places with faint lines. Not natural. Etched. Spirals within spirals.

Time stretched thin.

Or looped.

She couldn't tell how long they'd been walking, only that her legs ached and her hands were trembling.

Then the trees broke open.

———

The clearing was a perfect circle.

Dead silent.

Not a bird. Not a rustle.

The trees formed a tight, gnarled wall around it—saplings with thick trunks and pale bark, their branches bare but shivering in a wind that didn't touch her skin.

At the center stood a structure.

Sloane had no name for it.

It looked sick, like it had been grown instead of built—twisted from root and stone, rising no higher than a one-story building, but sinking deep. Its top sagged like a collapsed lung, and its base was split with a dark opening. A tunnel mouth.

Not a door.

A throat.

It pulsed faintly in the fog.

Sloane stepped forward.

The air around the structure shimmered—not with heat, but with something else, like light distorted by grief.

She touched the stone.

It was warm. And wet.

Like skin.

She pulled her hand back.

Cal's voice came low behind her.

"This is it."
"This is the Root."

———

Sloane's chest felt tight.

Like the air inside the clearing was heavier than the rest of the forest.

"Tell me what happened," she said. "The first time."

Cal's hands were clenched at his sides.

"They brought me here blindfolded," he said. "Told me it was tradition. Told me it would make me strong. I was sixteen."

His voice cracked.

"They led me down inside. Just for a moment. Just long enough to feel it."

"What did you see?"

He met her eyes.

"I don't know."

A pause.

"But I haven't heard silence since."

Chapter 23
Into the Root

The mouth of The Root gaped wide at the base of the spiral clearing, slick with condensation and ringed in lichen that glowed faintly in the low light.

It wasn't a door.

It was a wound.

A dark, open seam in the earth—breathing slow and damp. The stone around it was porous and slick, laced with a fine layer of moss that pulsed slightly when Sloane touched it.

Alive.

Still warm from something that had passed through.

Or something still waiting inside.

She looked back at Cal. He stood silent, his face unreadable, as if already halfway underground.

Sloane ducked low, pressed her hands to the lip of the tunnel, and crawled in.

The air inside changed instantly.

Gone was the cool morning breeze, the scent of pine needles and rain.

Here, it was wet and sour, thick as fog. Every breath came heavy with the smell of rotting wood, rusted iron, and something sweet beneath it, like syrup turned to vinegar.

The walls were slick, pulsing with root clusters that shivered when her hand brushed them.

Her flashlight stuttered once.

Then held.

The beam swept forward across packed earth, low ceilings, and roots that hung like tendons, slick with sap the color of old blood.

Beneath her palms, the tunnel floor was no longer dirt.

It was spongy.

A strange, velvet-slick texture that made her recoil, then keep crawling. It squished faintly under her weight—like something that had once been soft, then spoiled.

Behind her, Cal's voice came low.

"Do you hear that?"

Sloane froze.

And then she did.

A sound—not loud, not obvious. But present.

A pulse.

Low, steady, deep—like the echo of a heartbeat carried through stone.

Not human.

Not near.

But everywhere.

———

The tunnel sloped downward in a tight spiral.

As they moved, Sloane's sense of distance distorted. Her shoulders brushed the walls now. Her back scraped the ceiling. She felt like she was moving through the throat of something huge, and it was slowly closing around her.

Her watch flickered. Then went blank.

Time bent.

Minutes stretched like molasses down a drain.

And then—suddenly—they dropped into a chamber.

———

It was round, low-ceilinged, and wet.

The walls were stone, but not clean—scratched, gouged, marked with thousands of illegible carvings. No symmetry. No pattern. Just chaos.

Except in one place.

Directly across the chamber, etched into the wall in deliberate lines: a spiral. Clean. Repeating. Tightening until it ended in a single, still-wet word:

HER

Sloane's breath caught.

Then her light passed over the center of the room—and stopped.

A basin sat there.

Stone-carved. Waist-high. Wide and smooth and deeply wrong.

It was filled to the rim with black water, thick as oil. Perfectly still. It did not reflect. It did not ripple. It only *waited.*

Above it, hanging from the ceiling like a sentinel, was a carving of the Pine Siskin.

Wings folded.

Beak wide open.

And set deep into its carved face: a blood-red stone, where the eye should be.

The only one she had ever seen intact.

The whole room seemed to vibrate around it.

———

Sloane approached the basin slowly, heart thudding.

The smell of the water hit first—earth and iron and something coppery, like raw meat wrapped in silk.

She leaned forward.

Raised her flashlight.

And saw it.

A face.

Just beneath the surface. Motionless.

A girl's face.

Pale. Eyes wide open. Mouth frozen in a silent scream that never broke the surface.

Delia.

Sloane stumbled back with a gasp, slamming into Cal.

The water didn't move.

Didn't even tremble.

It just held her reflection beside Delia's.

Like it wanted her there, too.

———

Cal stood still.

His flashlight shaking slightly in his hand.

"I thought she was gone," Sloane whispered.

"She's not gone," Cal said.

Sloane turned to him, voice shaking.

"You said you didn't remember what happened the second time you came down here."

His eyes were locked on the basin.

"You said you blacked out."

His jaw clenched.

"Said you didn't know what was inside."

The light flickered overhead.

He didn't look at her.

His voice came softer than a breath, barely human.

"I lied."

———

Silence.

A long, slow, stretching silence—so wide it swallowed every sound.

Then:

"They made me watch."
"They said the seals only held if someone gave it their eyes. Their memory. A tether."

He turned to her then.

His face was gray. Ashen. A boy who had once looked inside the truth and never recovered.

"I saw her. Just like that.
I saw her face for years every time I closed my eyes.
But I couldn't say her name. I couldn't speak about it.
I didn't just lie to you, Sloane…"

A breath.

"I lied to myself."

Sloane looked down at the basin again.

And this time—

The water rippled.

Chapter 24
The Reflection That Speaks

The ripple was slight.

Just a shimmer across the basin's inky surface—one widening ring, spreading outward from the center like a dropped pin in still water.

Then another.

And another.

Each one perfectly spaced. Calm. Intentional.

Sloane stood at the edge of the stone basin, her breath shallow, the beam of her flashlight hovering just over the surface. It didn't reflect. It swallowed. Like the water wasn't water at all, but a mouth open in permanent silence.

She leaned closer.

Not because she wanted to.
Because she had to.

The water beneath her glowed with an oily sheen, and through it—Delia's face still floated, suspended in stillness, pale as bone and eerily untouched by time. Eyes open. Mouth frozen in the shape of a scream.

But not a scream of terror.

A scream of witnessing.

———

The chamber around them was low and round, the air stale and damp. Walls of ancient stone bled moisture in thin, glistening veins, feeding the tangled roots that threaded through the room like veins inside a creature too large to name.

Every surface was marked.

Not carved—scratched. Torn. Clawed.

The symbols had no order. They looped over one another, old language and new, spirals buried in spirals, until the stone looked almost soft with repetition.

The ceiling pulsed faintly above them, where the Pine Siskin carving hung like a watchful eye. Its wings were curled inward, like it had folded them in prayer or surrender. Its beak hung wide. From the socket of its eye, a dull red stone stared down—too deep in color to be glass, too smooth to be raw.

It gleamed wetly.

Like it had been weeping something dark.

———

Cal said nothing. He hadn't since they entered.

He stood just behind her, barely breathing, the flashlight on his chest flickering as if caught in a slow, steady wind—though the chamber held no draft.

Then came the sound.

Not a sound, exactly.

A feeling.

Like pressure against her ribs.

A deep, steady vibration that crawled through the soles of her boots and up her spine. It pulsed in rhythm—not like a drum, but like a heart-beat the size of the forest above them.

Then the whisper came.

Not loud.

Not even in the air.

It vibrated through the stone. Through her bones. Through her skull.

"She saw."

Sloane flinched, backing away from the basin—but the voice followed her.

"She saw.
She listened.
She remembered."

It was layered.

Not a voice.

Voices.

Multiple.

Woven together into something hollow and vast, as if the Root itself had learned how to speak.

She turned to Cal, voice shaking.

"You said you didn't remember what happened when you came here before."

He didn't respond.

He was staring into the basin now, wide-eyed, trembling.

She took a step toward him.

"You said you blacked out."

Another step.

"You said you didn't see what was inside."

He blinked once.

The tear that rolled down his cheek caught in the beam of his light like glass.

"I lied."

———

The words cracked something open in the room.

The walls seemed to lean inward.

The moisture thickened.

The pulse grew louder.

Cal's voice was hoarse now, his hands clenched into fists.

"I told them she wasn't right for it. She wasn't one of us. But they didn't care. They said it needed someone… young. Curious. Someone the Root would notice."

Sloane's stomach turned.

"You brought her."

"I loved her."
The words were a whisper, barely audible. "And I brought her."

He sank against the wall, sliding to the ground.

"I didn't know what they meant by *anchor.* I thought it meant something symbolic. Not…"

His eyes lifted to hers, bloodshot and distant.

"Not that they would put her in it."

———

The basin rippled again.

Delia's face began to change.

She blinked.

Once.

Then again.

Her mouth opened wider.

And the reflection began to move.

Not her body.

The water.

It swirled, slowly at first, then faster, the spiral tightening beneath the surface like a drain pulling inward—and as it did, the light in the room dimmed. Not from power. Not from shadows.

From memory.

Like the chamber was slipping back through time, pulling something forward.

And then—

A voice.

Not from the basin.

From behind them.

"I remember you."

Chapter 25
What Remains

The voice came from behind them.

Not loud.

Not sharp.

It *slid* into the room, curling through the chamber like smoke beneath a closed door—soft, wet, and inexplicably near.

"I remember you."

Sloane turned slowly.

Her flashlight beam trembled as it caught movement.

There—standing at the far edge of the chamber where stone bled into darkness—was Delia.

But not the Delia from the photo in the file. Not the one on the tape. Not the girl they'd remembered.

This Delia looked like she had been drawn from memory, her edges blurred slightly, her skin pale with a luminous sheen, as if dipped in wax. Damp hair hung around her face in matted strands, and her eyes—wide, hollow, still—reflected no light at all.

She didn't breathe.

Didn't blink.

But she looked through them as if she had never stopped.

Cal staggered back, stumbling into the wall. The beam from his chest light flared across Delia's face, catching in the hollow of her cheeks and the reflective gleam of her damp skin.

"You brought me here," she said.

———

Her voice was soft but sharp—like a whisper that had learned to cut through stone. It carried too far for the size of the room, reaching the edges like it remembered how sound was *supposed* to work.

Cal's lips parted, but no words came.

He looked shattered.

Sloane stepped forward before he could speak. Her heart thundered behind her ribs, each beat feeling too slow.

"Delia?" she asked.

Delia blinked once.
Not slowly.
Mechanically.

Like a mimic of movement.

"I heard you," she said, tilting her head slightly. "When you played the tape. When you touched the seal. When you stepped inside."

The moisture along the walls thickened, threading the carvings in dark rivulets. Roots twitched near the ceiling. The air pressed in, hot and tight and wet—like the inside of a sleeping throat.

"You were the voice," Sloane said.

"I was still forming," Delia replied. "Still *learning*. The Root remembers in shapes first. Sound comes later."

Cal made a sound. A choked half-breath.

He stepped toward her, flashlight swinging wildly.

"You're not real," he said. "You're not—this isn't real."

Delia's eyes slid toward him.

Her gaze sharpened.

"You brought me here," she said again.

"And then you left me."

The light from Sloane's hand passed over her again—and this time she could see it.

The seams.

Fine, glistening lines where Delia's body wasn't entirely whole. Her skin looked stitched together by memory and root. Her outline pulsed faintly with the same low rhythm they'd felt in the walls.

She wasn't solid.

But she wasn't ghost either.

She was something else.

Cal dropped to his knees, his voice breaking apart.

"I told them… she wasn't part of the old families. She wasn't meant for the spiral. I didn't know they were going to—" He swallowed hard. "They said it needed someone who could anchor it. Someone *pure*. Someone *young*."

He looked up.

Tears streamed down his cheeks.

"I loved you."

———

Delia's head tilted again.

Her expression didn't change.

She stepped forward, and the air around her bent—like she carried her own gravity, pulling everything toward her in silence.

Sloane reached out, blocking Cal from taking another step.

Delia's smile was almost imperceptible.

But it was there.

"I didn't ask to be the anchor," she said. "I just wanted to know the truth."

The basin behind them rippled again, this time without movement, without sound. Just a sudden shift in the air, like the chamber itself shuddered.

Delia turned her gaze to it.

And then—back to Sloane.

"You opened the door," she said.
"You asked the questions."
"And now something else is *waking up*."

———

The spiral on the wall began to glow—a faint red pulse leaking from the carved lines like fresh blood under skin. The word *HER* shimmered as droplets formed and fell to the floor below.

A heartbeat thumped in the silence.

Then again.

Slower now.

Stronger.

The lights flickered.

And from the basin, a shape began to rise.

Not Delia.

Something larger.

But before it fully formed, Delia stepped into the light.

Her voice dropped to a whisper, close, intimate.

Just for Sloane.

"The Root isn't a prison."
"It's a church."
"And I was the first one to pray."

Chapter 26
The Cradle Beneath

The basin behind Delia rippled again, the surface trembling in tight concentric rings. But it wasn't the kind of ripple that came from movement.

It came from response.

The Root was listening.

And now, it wanted to be heard.

The air in the chamber thickened—humid, sour, laced with the scent of wet roots and something deeper beneath it, something raw and metallic, like the inside of a wound that hadn't stopped bleeding.

Sloane felt it crawl into her lungs.

Cal stumbled to his feet, his flashlight swinging, light cutting over the stone walls. The carvings those thousands of ragged marks—had begun to shift.

Not literally.

But visually.

In the flickering beams, they seemed to move beneath the surface, like something trapped in the stone was pressing against the other side.

Sloane looked toward the basin again.

The water had gone still, but the blackness inside had taken on depth.

Like a drop of ink in clear liquid, slowly blooming into something vast and unreadable.

Delia stood still beside it, her face illuminated by the red-pulse glow now bleeding softly from the spiral wall.

"It's spreading," she said.

Her voice was quiet, reverent.

Sloane's throat tightened. "The Root?"

Delia nodded once.

"It's always been hungry. You just gave it your name."

———

The stone beneath Sloane's boots felt warmer now. Not hot, but charged—vibrating softly, the way a struck tuning fork hums against the skin.

Cal backed toward the tunnel, eyes darting to the ceiling, to the thick roots twisting there like tangled nerves. One of them twitched as he passed, curling minutely toward him.

"We need to go," he said.

"We can't," Sloane whispered.

"We should never have come," he hissed.

Delia stepped forward.

Just one step.

The air around her shimmered again.

Not like heat.

Like grief.

"You'll go," she said, "but it'll follow."

Her eyes turned toward Sloane, locking onto her with unnerving clarity.

"Because it remembers you now."

They left the chamber slowly.

Neither of them spoke as they crawled back up through the spiral tunnel, their flashlights dimming slightly as if the Root resisted their exit. The walls pressed in tighter. The roots seemed to multiply—twitching softly as they passed, whispering secrets in a language neither of them could understand.

By the time they emerged into the clearing above, the sky had changed.

It was no longer morning.

It wasn't evening either.

The air had gone golden-gray, the sun visible but smudged, like a fingerprint dragged across the sky. Clouds circled low and fast, too fast for weather.

And the trees…

The trees were all leaning now.

Sloane stood slowly, blinking up at them.

What had once looked like the natural curve of the spiral now looked more like submission—as if the forest had begun to bow inward toward a center it could no longer resist.

Cal wiped dirt from his arms, his voice shaking.

"I came here before. I left. But it didn't follow me then."

"You weren't its tether," Sloane said quietly.

He looked at her.

"You think I am now?"

She didn't answer.

Because something inside her already knew.

———

Back at Cabin 17, her father was waiting on the porch.

He wasn't sitting.

He was standing.

Still. Straight.

And afraid.

When Sloane stepped up the stairs, he looked at her like he didn't recognize her.

Or like he did—and hadn't expected to.

"I saw her," he whispered.

She stopped.

"Saw who?"

His eyes were wide. Wet. Locked on something behind her.

"Delia," he said. "But she wasn't Delia anymore."

He reached out, his fingers trembling.

"The Root's pulling at the seams."

———

That night, the spiral made its first appearance on the surface.

It was carved into the bark of a tree outside Cabin 9.

Fresh. Precise.

No one claimed to have done it.

But the bark was bleeding.

And somewhere far down in the earth beneath the cabins—

The Root remembered its next name.

Cabin Zero

Chapter 27
Signs Above Ground

The spiral appeared overnight.

Etched into the bark of an old pine outside Cabin 9, just a few feet from where the gravel path turned toward the lake. The morning light hadn't fully broken through the mist, so it glowed faintly in the pale wash of dawn—*deep, clean, deliberate.*

The cut was fresh.

Sap oozed slowly from the grooves, thick and amber, glinting where the light touched it. The symbol was precise—about the size of a dinner plate—drawn in smooth curves that ended in a sharp inward hook. The spiral curled tightly at its center, not like a flourish, but like a seal.

Sloane stood before it, wrapped in her jacket, her breath misting in the still air. The pine needles above barely moved. No birdsong. No wind. Just the sound of a single droplet of sap falling to the leaves below with a wet, tick.

The trees surrounding the marked pine leaned subtly inward, their branches heavy with morning condensation. Dew clung to every surface—railing, mailbox, even the edge of the porch swing nearby, giving the whole clearing a suspended, untouched feel, like the moment right before the first footstep in fresh snow.

Cal crouched beside the tree, gloved fingers brushing lightly over the spiral. He didn't press—just touched the edges of the symbol where the bark had curled slightly away from the pressure of the cut.

"Too straight for a knife," he murmured. "Too clean for any tool I've used."

Sloane knelt beside him, her knees pressing into the damp pine mulch. Her eyes followed the etched line.

"It's not carved," she said. "It's written."

———

Cabin 9 loomed nearby, its porch wrapped in overgrown ivy and morning shadow. The curtains were drawn tight, the porch lights still on despite the rising sun. A pair of ceramic boots sat near the front steps—planters once filled with begonias, now brittle and brown.

Sloane stepped toward the door, the wood creaking beneath her with every step. The air smelled like wet pine and the faintest trace of old cigarette smoke—someone had stood here recently.

Then the door cracked.

Just an inch.

Enough to show Mrs. Calhoun's face.

Her skin looked paper-thin, sagging gently beneath her eyes. A shawl wrapped tight around her shoulders. Her eyes—once sharp and bright from across town meetings and potlucks—now looked sunken, glassy with dread.

"Is it starting again?" she whispered.

Not hopeful. Not curious.

Resigned.

Sloane nodded.

And the door closed, gently.

Not with panic.

With understanding.

———

The fog held over town like it had been *laid there*, flat and still.

By noon, the breeze hadn't returned. The trees no longer rustled. Main Street sat in a strange hush, like every sound was being absorbed by the air itself.

Shops were open, but quiet.

The bakery's chalkboard menu hadn't been updated—just yesterday's specials fading in the light. The bell above Birdie's door didn't ring once. The usual chatter from porch rockers was absent. Even the dog that usually barked from the back of the mercantile didn't make a sound.

It was like Pine Hollow had paused.

Not out of fear.

Out of reverence.

———

By late afternoon, a second mark appeared.

On Cabin 12.

Not on the door. Not in the wood.

On the stone.

Sloane and Cal stood in the narrow path behind it, where the foundation met the slope toward the forest line. The spiral was etched just beneath a water spout, where rain left streaks in the concrete. This one was deeper—cut into the stone like it had always been there.

At its center: a dot.

Small.

Singular.

Like an eye.

Sloane reached out, fingertips brushing the edges.

It was warm.

And the stone hummed.

———

That evening, the woods grew darker before sunset.

The light filtered strangely through the trees, casting the cabins in shades of green and copper. Fog rolled low again, curling up the porch steps of each cabin like smoke from a fire that hadn't started yet.

Back at Cabin 17, her father stood on the porch. Still. Watching.

He hadn't moved in over an hour.

When Sloane stepped up beside him, he didn't look at her.

His hand rested flat against the porch post, fingertips twitching.

"Dad?" she asked softly.

His lips moved slowly.

"The seams are thinning."

She didn't ask what he meant.

Because she already knew.

———

That night, Sloane couldn't sleep.

She sat on the floor beside the window, knees pulled to her chest, watching the treetops lean in silhouette against the dim sky.

And just before midnight, the lights flickered—one by one, cabin by cabin.

A wave of pulsing amber across the resort, like breath moving through ribs.

From deep beneath the ground, she felt the hum again.

But this time it wasn't warning.

It was calling.

Chapter 28
The First to Go

The fog hadn't moved.

It clung low across the resort like it had settled in for good, swaddling the cabins in a soft, gray stillness. Trees stood like ghosts along the paths. The gravel didn't crunch beneath Sloane's boots—it muffled, damp and dark, pressing down with each careful step.

The morning had no birdsong.
No breeze.
Not even the steady whisper of the lake.

Just the occasional soft drip of condensation falling from a pine bough.

As if the woods were holding their breath.

She first saw the gathering near Cabin 4—two maintenance trucks parked crookedly in the grass, hazard lights still blinking like flashing warnings no one paid attention to. A thin line of yellow tape fluttered loosely between porch posts, sagging from dew, not tension.

Cal stood just outside the rope, jaw set, eyes darker than usual.

Sloane approached slowly.

"What happened?"

He didn't answer at first. Just stared past her, like whatever he saw had happened long before today.

"Kid's gone," he finally said.

Two words.

No explanation.
No disbelief.
Just truth. The kind that knows how to stand quietly in its own shadow.

———

The child's name was Owen McCay. Eight years old. Curious. Chatty. The kind of boy who carried a pocket magnifying glass to look at bugs and asked waitresses if ghosts were real.

He had come with his aunt. Weekend trip. Cabin 4.

His parents were two towns away, working an ER double shift.

His aunt had tucked him in around ten, checked the lock, cracked the window an inch to let in the pine-scented breeze.

She woke just before dawn.

Window wide open.

Bed empty.

Covers undisturbed.

No footprints on the floor. No muddy trail through the pines.
Just a scatter of pine needles on the sheet—

—and a spiral.

Drawn in faded green sidewalk chalk across the headboard.

Sloane stood just outside the cabin door, her hands in her coat pockets, heart beating slow and hollow as she watched the Association investigators comb through the room.

No one looked frantic.

No one looked surprised.

Just grim.

Like they'd been waiting for this.

The spiral was still visible—wobbly, imperfect, as if drawn by a child's hand but following a pattern it didn't understand. The chalk had begun to smear from the damp. But the lines remained legible.

Sloane didn't need to step inside to know.

It was the same spiral.

Same as the ones on the bark.
Same as the stone behind Cabin 12.

Only this time—

It wasn't a warning.

It was a signature.

Owen's aunt sat on the porch, arms wrapped around herself, a blanket draped over her lap though the air was warm enough to sweat. Her eyes were red. Her lips pale. She didn't look at Sloane when she passed, but she spoke as if she'd been waiting for her to listen.

"I didn't hear him leave."

Her voice was thin. Brittle.

"I always wake up when he rolls over. He kicks sometimes. But last night…" She trailed off.

Her gaze dropped to her hands.

"Last night I didn't hear anything."

———

Down the path, Caleb stood talking to two Association men in dark coats. They didn't wear badges, but they didn't need to. The way they moved—controlled, measured—told Sloane everything.

They weren't here to investigate.

They were here to contain.

Sloane joined them at the edge of the grass. Caleb didn't look at her.

He stared at the pine forest.

"I told them this would happen," he said. His voice was rough. Low. "I said the seals weren't holding. That the Root would want balance again."

She looked at him carefully.

"You said this thing doesn't take out of revenge."

He nodded once.

"It takes to remember."

———

The fog never burned off.

It thickened into evening.

Shadows stretched long and low across the paths, and porch lights flickered on without fanfare. Curtains stayed drawn. Radios silent. Even the lake, usually rippling with silver motion at sunset, looked like polished glass—still and waiting.

That night, Sloane walked the trail behind the cabins. The trees creaked gently in the windless dark. Not groaning—breathing.

And near the edge of the woods, she saw it.

A new spiral.

Carved into the base of a tree not twenty feet from Cabin 4.

Smaller than the others.

But deeper.

Etched not in chalk, but with something sharp. Bark curled from its edges in tiny shavings that still clung to the roots below.

And in the very center of the spiral—

A dot.

A single, perfect impression.

Like an eye had opened.

And looked back.

Chapter 29
The Memory That Isn't Yours

Sloane didn't remember falling asleep.

One moment she was curled on the rug in front of the fire, watching the last logs collapse into glowing coals—their heat dimming in slow pulses like a heart in its final hour—and the next...

Mist.

Thick and silver-blue, curling around her ankles, her wrists, her throat. The air hung heavy, not just with damp but with intention, as though the fog was deciding whether to let her through.

She opened her eyes, and the forest breathed around her.

But this was not Pine Hollow as she knew it.

The trees were taller, older. Their trunks arched like cathedral columns, bark slick and dark, laced with root-veins that pulsed faintly under the moss. The scent here was deeper—loam and rot, but also something sweet, like wildflower honey gone to ferment.

She looked down at her hands.

And they weren't hers.

The fingers were slender, callused from writing. Her sweatshirt sleeves were too short, frayed at the cuffs. A single, thin braid draped over her shoulder, tied with a string of faded red yarn.

Her breath hitched.

These weren't her hands.
This wasn't her body.

This was Delia's memory.

———

She turned slowly, her movements drawn along a path she hadn't chosen.

And there—half-lost in the fog, crouched against a slope of earth and tangled vine—stood a cabin.

Older than the others.

Sick with time.

Its shingles had rotted in jagged rows. A corner of the roof sagged in defeat. Ivy wrapped the structure like a shroud, but at its crown, white blossoms bloomed—unseasonal, bright, and wide open as if watching.

A warped wooden sign hung above the door, the paint flaked but still legible:

CABIN 0.

Delia moved toward it.

So did Sloane.

Their feet were the same.

Their heartbeat was the same.

———

The door creaked open before she touched it, revealing a single-room interior thick with shadow and the faint, choking scent of mildew. No windows. Just a soft, golden lantern hanging from the rafters, swaying gently on a rusted hook.

The floor moaned beneath her.

Not from weight.

From memory.

A basin stood in the center of the room.

Wide. Carved from dark stone.

And filled not with water, but ink—black, viscous, slowly rippling in slow circles like it remembered how to breathe.

Delia stepped forward.

Sloane felt it in her knees, her shoulders, her neck—the strain of choice wrapped in inevitability.

———

Reflected in the basin's surface: Delia's face.

Not frightened.

Not blank.

Resigned.

Sixteen, maybe seventeen. Eyes wide, wary but clear. A girl who had asked too many questions. Who had read things she shouldn't have. Who knew that stepping into the spiral was not an accident—it was the cost of curiosity.

And behind her, they emerged.

Figures.

Tall. Clean. Coats buttoned high. Faces indistinct, smoothed by fog and forgetting. Hands behind their backs. They watched, not like observers, but architects. One held a book. Another lit a taper, not to see—but to mark the moment.

A woman's voice—sharp and low:

"The Root needs presence."
"She's seen enough to bind."
"Let it take her."

———

Delia spoke then.

Sloane felt her mouth move. The words came with a tremor.

"You said I'd *see,* not *stay.*"

A pause. Heavy. Final.

The voice again:

"All memory has a price."

The spiral on the floor began to glow beneath her feet—red first, then gold, then black again, sinking into the wood like ink bleeding through paper.

Delia looked down at the basin.

And then up—

Right into Sloane's eyes.

"Don't let them tell my story wrong."

———

Sloane gasped awake.

The fire had burned down to powder and ash.

The air in the cabin felt too still.

Too exact.

The silence wrapped around her like a second skin.

She sat up slowly, heart hammering, sweat drying on the back of her neck.

And then she saw it.

Drawn faintly in green chalk on her wrist—

A spiral.

Perfectly shaped.

Still wet to the touch.

Chapter 3Ø
The Association's Hand

The chalk spiral had mostly faded by morning.

Sloane stood at the bathroom sink, the tap running warm as she held her wrist under the stream. The water curved around her skin, soft and soundless, washing away the last of the green dust—but the shape lingered beneath the surface.

Even when it was gone, she could still feel it.

As if it had soaked deeper than skin.

Drawn into her like memory.

She turned off the water.

Listened.

The cabin creaked faintly in its joints. The low murmur of wind outside. The tick of the kitchen clock.

Nothing else.

Cal hadn't knocked.

And she hadn't decided whether that was good or bad.

———

By the time she reached town, the sun had technically risen—but you'd never know it.

The fog still clung to the earth like a second skin, coiled tight around porch steps and tree trunks, softening edges, muting the world. The road was damp and dark, and every footstep she took felt too loud, like a stranger in her own shoes.

Main Street was open—but sleepwalking.

Birdie's bakery windows were dark.

The bookstore's bell was silenced with a strip of fabric.

Even the American flag outside the town office didn't move, though the air carried just enough cold to lift hair from her neck.

No birds. No music. No chatter.

Just the stillness of a town that had heard something *move* and was pretending it hadn't.

———

She saw Nora Mercer before she heard her.

Standing alone near the chapel steps, under the awning's curve of wood and shadow, as still as a painting.

Wool coat buttoned. Hair twisted back in a perfect, pale coil. Black gloves clasped neatly at her waist. The expression of a woman who knew exactly what she came to say—and how she wanted to be heard.

Sloane stepped onto the gravel.

Nora turned.

Not in greeting.

In acknowledgment.

"I thought you might come," she said.

Her voice, as always, was glass-smooth.

Sloane stopped four feet from her, the mist curling between them.

"Did you know what they did to her?"

No formalities.

Nora didn't blink.

"I knew what they offered her."

"You didn't answer my question."

A pause.

The slow tilt of her chin.

Then:

"Yes."

———

The word hung in the air like smoke.

Sloane felt it settle in her lungs, acidic and real.

They stood beneath the chapel's overhang, the carved Pine Siskin perched above them in its wooden halo, head tilted mid-song—but no sound came.

Nora's voice lowered a notch. Still clear. Still cold.

"She was asking too many questions. Reading the old minutes. Poking through the archives at the Preservation Society. She came to me. Said she wanted to understand the spiral. Said she felt... called."

"She was a teenager."

"She was seventeen. She asked. She agreed."

Sloane stepped forward, gravel crunching.

"She didn't agree to disappear."

"She agreed to remember," Nora said.

"And the cost?"

"All memory has one."

———

A silence passed between them, long and weighty as thunder not yet heard.

Then Nora moved—reaching into her coat pocket, pulling out a thin, battered folder. She offered it like a peace offering. Or a threat.

Sloane took it.

Her hands trembled as she opened it.

Inside, pages aged to the color of weak tea, edges curled and soft. A meeting header stamped in red across the top.

Association Emergency Minutes
Subject: Spiral Instability / Candidate Options

She read the names.

Nora Mercer.
Jack Wren.
Ellis Hart.
Two others she didn't know.

The date: Twelve years ago.

Delia Harper's name appeared four times.

Each time beside the same phrase:

"Candidate: Memory Vessel (non-family line)."

———

Sloane's breath caught.

Her father's handwriting scrawled in the margin of one page:

"This isn't binding. It's burial."

She looked up at Nora.

"You used her."

Nora's gaze didn't shift.

"We *needed* her."

"She was an orphan."

"She was *available*."

Sloane's voice cracked. "And disposable."

"She was *effective*." Nora's words came with frost. "And now, so are you."

———

The wind stirred faintly then.

Just enough to shift a curl of mist past Nora's boots.

She turned to go, already done with the conversation.

But just before she stepped off the porch, she paused.

Gloved hand on the railing.

Voice low and polished, like every word had been ironed flat.

"Your father tried to stop it."
"But in the end—he chose you, too."

Cabin Zero

Chapter 31
Cabin Zero Cracks

Cabin Zero no longer looked abandoned.

It looked watched.

The trees leaned toward it now—not dramatically, not enough to alarm—but in the way people lean toward someone whispering. The vines that once clung lazily to the siding had thickened overnight, twisting upward like rope pulled by invisible hands. The boards along the porch steps had begun to split at the edges, not from rot, but from pressure—as if something beneath had started to push upward.

Sloane stood at the edge of the path, the mist clinging to her ankles, pine needles damp beneath her boots.

Beside her, Cal said nothing.

His breath clouded in the cool air, but the wind was still.

Not a single bird sang.

And the door was already ajar.

It creaked open when Sloane stepped onto the porch.

Not loudly.

Like a sigh from a mouth too tired to speak.

The air inside the cabin hit her like a wave—warm, wet, metallic, tinged with mildew and the faint copper-sweet tang of blood that had dried and been washed away and dried again. The kind of scent that clung behind the ears. The kind that told the truth even when everyone else lied.

Her flashlight clicked on with a thin beam of white.

The interior looked smaller than before. Closer.

The walls didn't just hold carvings now. They wore them.

———

Where once there had been a single spiral—carefully etched into the paneling—there were now dozens, maybe hundreds, layered and tangled like vines competing for sunlight. Carved deep, splintering the grain, the lines jagged and furious.

Some spirals were small and tucked into corners. Others stretched nearly from floor to ceiling, as if whoever made them couldn't stop once they'd started.

Sloane stepped closer.

Each spiral had a word beneath it—scratched like a signature.

Not *Delia.*

Not *Her.*

Just one word, over and over:

You.

She turned slowly, the beam of her light following the curve of the room.

The basin was gone.

———

Where it had once stood, proud and ancient, there was now only a blackened ring scorched into the wood. The boards around it had cracked outward in a perfect radial pattern—like impact, or emergence.

Cal knelt beside it, running his fingers lightly over the edge.

"Burned," he murmured. "From the inside."

The wood flaked like charred paper under his touch.

A thin curl of smoke lifted from the center.

No heat.

No flame.

Just the slow exhale of memory coming undone.

———

Then Sloane saw it.

At the base of the far wall—just beside the lowest spiral—the wood had split.

Not from age.

From force.

A jagged crack had opened between the floorboards and the paneling, revealing dirt below. The floor had buckled slightly around it, warping like something had pushed up, stretching the structure until it fractured.

And in the dirt:

A root.

Pale as bone, thin as a finger. Coiled. Still.

Until it moved.

———

Sloane froze.

Cal stepped beside her, flashlight trained on the hole.

The root didn't retract.

It twitched again—curling, not like a plant, but like something alive and learning how to stretch.

Sloane crouched slowly, bringing her face closer to the floor. The air radiating from the crack was different—wet, iron-rich, like a cave where something had been buried, then changed its mind.

She reached out—just her fingertips brushing the edge of the floorboard.

The boards were warm.

And beneath her hand, the faintest sound:

Ba-dump. Ba-dump. Ba-dump.

A heartbeat.

Not hers.

Not Cal's.

The cabin's.

———

"This isn't a chamber anymore," Cal whispered, as if speaking louder might wake it fully.

Sloane nodded, her mouth dry.

"It's not even a room."

"Then what is it?"

She looked up at the walls.

At the spirals that stared back.

At the word carved beneath them all: *You.*

"It's a mouth," she said.
"And it's learning how to say my name."

Chapter 32
Fire at the Edge

The smoke found her before the sound did.

Sloane woke coughing, eyes stinging, the air inside Cabin 17 already laced with the scent—not of pine, not of campfire, but something darker. Acrid and sweet. Like burnt plastic, or memories catching flame.

She was on her feet in seconds, heart pounding in her throat.

Orange light flickered against the windows.

Not sunrise.

Fire.

She was out the door in boots and an unzipped coat, the flashlight cold in her hand, breath pluming in short bursts as she sprinted through the dark.

She didn't need to ask where.

She already knew.

The flames danced low and clean across the slope near the lake.

Cabin 3 was collapsing inward, its frame glowing like coals, the roof already caved in. Fire coiled up through the rafters, licking at them like something hungry—but not out of control.

This fire wasn't wild.

It was precise.

———

Three Association men stood nearby. Their coats unmarked, their expressions unreadable. No one shouted orders. No one called for help. They just watched the cabin burn like it was part of the schedule.

Birdie was there too, wrapped in a shawl, arms folded over her chest, bare feet dusted with soot. Her coffee mug steamed in the orange light, untouched.

"They said it was lightning," she murmured as Sloane stepped beside her.

"There wasn't a storm," Sloane said.

"I know."

Birdie's gaze didn't move.

"It smells like burning teeth."

———

The fire didn't spread. It didn't reach the trees. It didn't endanger the cabins nearby.

It did what it came to do.

Just before sunrise, the last beam snapped and folded into the ashes.

One of the Association men turned off the water with a nod, like he'd just finished hosing down a sidewalk.

And that was that.

Sloane came back alone, hours later, once the smoke had thinned and the men had gone.

Ash whispered beneath her boots. The ground steamed faintly. The cabin was gone, a blackened outline stamped into the soil. She moved slowly through what was left—past melted hinges and blistered siding, past beams turned skeletal and soft.

Something glinted near the foundation.

She crouched.

Brushed away the soot with the edge of her sleeve.

A metal nameplate, bent and blackened, edges curled from heat.

She lifted it, and the name stared back at her:

JACK WREN, DETECTIVE – PINE HOLLOW

Her breath caught.

She hadn't seen this before.

Not in the box. Not in the cabin.

But it was real. Heavy in her palm. Familiar in the worst way.

Like a part of him had survived the fire just long enough to make sure she saw it.

Cal joined her, stepping carefully around the beam fragments.

"That's from his old desk," he said quietly. "The one before the remodel."

"I didn't even know it still existed."

He crouched beside her.

"They weren't supposed to keep anything."

Sloane turned the plate over.

Her fingers froze.

There—scratched into the underside, deep and erratic—was a spiral.

Not clean. Not ceremonial.

Desperate.

Like someone had carved it fast, knowing they wouldn't get another chance.

————

She stood slowly, the plate still in her hand.

Looked out at the trees.

And there—just beyond the fire line, in the low brush near Cabin Zero—a thin coil of smoke.

Not from timber.

From earth.

————

Cal stepped beside her.

"You hear that?" he asked.

She listened.

Nothing.

And then—soft, low, nearly inaudible—

A creaking.

Like old beams shifting.

Or breath rising through soil.

————

Sloane tightened her grip on the nameplate, the edge biting into her palm.

"They didn't burn him," she said quietly.

Cal turned to her.

"They tried to bury him?"

"No." Her voice was a whisper now. A truth uncovered.

"They tried to erase where he stood."

Chapter 33
One More Door

By the time the sunlight hit the bakery windows, Birdie was already gone.

Not missing.

Gone.

The kind of gone Pine Hollow knew too well.

The kind that didn't leave blood or struggle or answers.
Just air that felt too still.
Just corners that held the memory of someone who used to stand in them.

———

Sloane stood outside the bakery at 8:04 a.m., one hand wrapped around a paper cup that had long gone cold. The sign on the door was flipped to *Closed*, but that wasn't strange for a Sunday morning.

What was strange were the windows.

Bare. Uncurtained.
No wreaths. No chalk hearts. No tiny wooden Pine Siskins perched along the sill.

Just the slow condensation of morning breath on glass.

And silence.

Too much of it.

———

She reached for the knob.

It turned easily.

Unlocked.

The bell above the door gave a weak jingle as she stepped inside, the sound swallowed almost instantly by the quiet.

The bakery felt... folded.

Not abandoned. Not chaotic. Just put away. Like Birdie had tucked everything back into its place for the last time, smoothed the edges of her life flat, and vanished.

The lights were off.
The ovens cold.
The warmth gone, but not long gone.

The air still held traces of what she had been baking last—something lemony, something soft. It clung to the floorboards like perfume after someone's left the room.

Sloane moved slowly, her boots tapping softly on the black-and-white tile.

———

Past the counter.

Past the empty pastry case.

To the low shelf under the register, half-concealed by a folded tea towel printed with tiny pinecones.

And there it was.

A small square of paper.

Not tucked away.
Placed.

Her name written across the top:

SLOANE

Block letters.

Written in black ink with the kind of pressure that meant every stroke was a decision.

Her breath caught as she unfolded it.

No greeting.

No signature.

Just three lines.

There's another door.
But it only opens for the right name.
Don't speak it unless you're sure.

———

Sloane read it again.

The words were ordinary.

The weight behind them wasn't.

She could still see Birdie's eyes from the night before—glassy, distant, lit by firelight from the hill above Cabin 3. Not afraid. Not panicked.

Prepared.

Like she'd already handed off her part of the story.

And now it was up to Sloane to decide whether to keep turning pages.

———

She turned toward the back of the bakery.

There was no kitchen noise. No water running. No humming. No ceramic clinks from Birdie cleaning up.

Just the faint creak of wood settling.

And through the window above the sink, the trees looked closer than they had the day before. The trail that ran behind the bakery, half-swallowed by underbrush and time, was darker now.

Not just shaded.

Waiting.

———

Cal met her at the edge of the gravel lot, his hair still damp from a rushed shower, boots unlaced.

"You went in?"

"She's not there."

"You're sure?"

She held up the note.

He took it without a word, reading it slowly, lips moving with each line.

When he finished, he folded it once, then handed it back like it might bite.

"She knew where the next door was," he said.

Sloane nodded.

"She also knew that not all doors are meant to be opened."

———

They walked the path behind the bakery in silence.

The air grew cooler with every step.

The trees leaned closer. The underbrush thinned without parting. The light turned green-gray, like it filtered through memory instead of clouds.

Sloane didn't know how far they'd go.

But the note in her pocket pulsed against her thigh like a second heartbeat.

And deep ahead, past the last bend in the trail—

The woods made room for something.

Not a door.

Not yet.

But the idea of one.

And whatever it opened onto—

Knew she was coming.

Chapter 34
The Story That Binds

The Pine Hollow Preservation Society always felt too clean.

Like memory had been scrubbed and shelved.

Sloane pushed open the tall oak door and stepped inside. The bell above her jingled—not a cheerful ring, but a brittle chime, like it didn't want to echo too loudly.

The air smelled of waxed floors, aged pine, and old paper.

Faint. Familiar.

Like the inside of a sealed book that hadn't been opened in years.

The front room was empty.

No receptionist.
No murmurs of local historians.
No clink of tea cups from the reading table.

Just rows of displays catching dust motes in the still air.

She moved slowly past the exhibits she'd seen a dozen times—some even as a child visiting her father when he first started volunteering here:

• A shadow box of antique keys from the original cabins.

• A model of the town square, painstakingly recreated with scale storefronts and tiny lamp posts.

• And the town's motto carved into polished pine beneath a mounted Pine Siskin:

We Remember What Matters.

The bird's wings were spread mid-flight, but its head was turned—looking backward.

———

The light through the stained-glass windows bled across the hardwood floor in muted colors: moss green, amber, and the pale, antique blue of winter sky. It painted the room in memory, not warmth.

Sloane's boots echoed softly as she moved past the public records area.

She knew where she needed to go.

To the back.

Where the sealed histories were kept.

———

The archivist's desk was abandoned. A cup of coffee sat cooling beside a stack of local event pamphlets. Half-drunk. No steam. A single pen rolled to the edge of the blotter pad, as if dropped mid-thought.

The lower drawer of the desk was open an inch.

Sloane didn't touch it.

She followed the trail—the footprints barely pressed into dust.

Boot soles. Clean. Small. Not hers.

They disappeared through the narrow arch into the archive.

***

The air changed instantly.

Cooler. Denser.
Like the room breathed different air than the rest of the building.

Motion sensors triggered dim overhead bulbs one by one—click—click—click—as she moved deeper into the stacks. The sound echoed off metal shelves and concrete walls, each light blinking on like a reluctant witness.

Here, the shelves weren't labeled with friendly markers or colored tags.

Just numbers.

Dates.

And red wax seals pressed into manila folders.

***

She moved past the genealogy files. Past the founding family correspondence. Past a row of shelves marked "Private Archives – Board Access Only."

Then she saw it.

Box 47. Slightly crooked. Dusty.

And stamped in heavy, blocky red ink:

EMERGENCY SESSION – JULY 13 – SPIRAL SUBJECT

She slid the box free, coughing as dust bloomed in the air.

It was heavier than it looked.

The kind of weight that didn't come from paper.

It came from what had been agreed to and forgotten.

———

She sat cross-legged on the cool stone floor and opened the lid.

Inside—carefully preserved, dated, and sorted—were meeting minutes, internal memos, and printed transcripts of confidential interviews. The pages were typed, but many bore handwritten notes in the margins. Some in red. Others in a familiar, sharp scrawl.

Her father's handwriting.

"Not containment. Reframing."
"This is about what's remembered—not what's true."
"If we bind the story, we bind the town."

Sloane flipped deeper into the file.

Delia's name appeared more than once.

Not as a victim. Not even as a subject.

As a solution.

One transcript jumped out:

> *"She's asking too much. Digging through the old names. The spiral's responding to her presence. She's attuned."*
> *"Is she willing?"*
> *"She believes she'll learn the truth."*

The margins were marked in red:

"A willing anchor is stronger."

Sloane's chest tightened.

They didn't pick her because she was dangerous.

They picked her because she wanted to know.

———

Beneath the stack was a thinner file.

Older.

Stamped in faded gray ink:

CATEGORY 1 – FORGETTING PROTOCOL – NARRATIVE INTERRUPTION

Inside: silence written on paper.

Instructions for severing storylines. Guidelines for redirecting memory through ritual, repetition, and misinformation. Notes about collective forgetting as a method of preserving order.

A line highlighted in green:

"Truth can be overwritten if the story is louder."

Her father had circled it.

Underneath, he wrote:

"Unless someone remembers it clearly. Then it becomes a fault line."

———

At the very bottom of the box, tucked between two brittle folders, was a cassette tape.

Old. Labeled in thick, blocky Sharpie:

J.W. – SPIRAL FRAGMENT – UNCUT

She stared at it for a long moment.

It was cool in her hand. The kind of cool that came from places no sunlight ever reached.

She didn't need to press play yet.

She knew what it was.

Not a goodbye.
Not instructions.
Not even protection.

A witness.

His voice—unscrubbed, unedited, unburied.

Because Jack Wren had seen what they were doing.

And he had chosen to remember anyway.

Chapter 35
What You Take With You

The clearing didn't appear on any map.

It didn't sit along a trail or behind a landmark. It wasn't bordered by signs or fencing. But Sloane had known where to find it the same way she had known the basin would be gone.

The spiral had led her here.

Not with arrows.

With memory.

The forest opened around her like a ribcage.

Pines leaned in from all sides, their trunks curved—not by storm, but by something older. Something beneath the roots that pulled.

Moss blanketed the ground, thick and soft and green-gray, broken only by the spiral.

Etched into the earth itself.

Not shallow.

Not recent.

Old. Worn smooth by time.

It stretched thirty feet wide, every line carved deep and true. Pine needles lay evenly along the ridges, not scattered, but placed—as if the forest itself had arranged them.

No wind touched them.

No insects stirred.

Only the quiet sound of breath not yet taken.

———

Sloane stepped into the spiral.

Cal followed, slower, reluctant. He stayed near the edge, his eyes locked on the trees.

They were watching.

Not with sight.

With memory.

———

The cassette in her coat pocket felt impossibly heavy.

The label worn smooth by her thumb.

J.W. – SPIRAL FRAGMENT – UNCUT

She hadn't listened yet.

Part of her had been afraid that if she did, it would change her.

But now she understood—it already had.

This story didn't start with her.

But it had been waiting for her.

She knelt in the very center of the spiral.

The moss was damp beneath her knees, springy and cool.

The air smelled of sap and wet stone and something beneath it—

Old ink.

Like the inside of a forgotten book.

She pulled out the cassette player—dusty, cracked, borrowed from the Society basement. Her fingers trembled as she clicked the tape into place.

The button stuck for a second.

Then depressed with a soft click.

For a moment, there was only hiss.

Then her father's voice.

Low. Rough. No greeting.

Just a man recording something he knew no one wanted to hear.

"If you're hearing this… then the spiral chose you, too."

"I tried to follow the rules. Tried to believe the Association knew what they were doing. But I kept seeing the holes. The edits. The names that disappeared from the records."

"Delia wasn't taken. She was given."

"They think if they control the story, they can control the Root. But the Root doesn't care about control."

"It cares about what's remembered."

The hiss returned.

Longer this time.

Then—

A second voice.

Faint.

Familiar.

Delia.

But not a recording.

Not echo.

Present.

"You found the fault line."

"You remembered the wrong thing."

"That means it remembers you, too."

———

The spiral beneath Sloane's knees began to warm.

Not from fire.

From recognition.

The moss shifted as if exhaling. Pine needles rolled gently outward from the center. The trees groaned, their branches stretching slowly inward, their trunks bending like ribs drawing closer to protect a heart.

Cal stepped forward. "Sloane—"

She didn't answer.

The tape clicked off.

And the clearing leaned closer.

She stood.

Closed her eyes.

And spoke the name.

Not whispered.

Not shouted.

Just true.

"Delia Harper."

The ground didn't shake.

The sky didn't split.

But the spiral pulsed.

A sound like wood cracking echoed through the clearing. The moss at the center blackened slightly, as if scorched from below.

Roots rose through the soil—slow, curling, deliberate.

A single point of light flickered near the edge of the trees.

Then a figure stepped forward.

Barefoot. Clothes too clean.

Eyes glassy. Distant.

Not Delia.

Not fully.

Someone new.

Not born.

Returned.

They moved slowly into the clearing, stopping just at the outer ring of the spiral. Their skin was pale. Their mouth slightly open, like they were on the edge of speech but didn't know the words.

And on their shoulder—

A fresh spiral scar.

Still pink. Still raised.

———

Sloane took one step forward.

Cal caught her wrist.

"Do you know them?"

"I think I will."

She looked down at the spiral beneath her feet.

The ridges still glowing faintly, as if the earth had just remembered how to feel.

———

She understood now.

The spiral didn't take to punish.

It took to preserve.

Stories lost. Voices silenced. Truths buried.

It had never wanted sacrifice.

It wanted someone who could hold it.

Someone who would speak the name.

———

Sloane looked up.

The trees didn't move.

The wind didn't rise.

But deep beneath the soil—

Something was listening.

Not to hurt.

Not to haunt.

But to make sure someone, somewhere, would remember.

* * *

End of Book One
Cabin Zero: Beneath The Pines

Cabin 17
Beneath the Surface

While caring for her father, an ex-detective, in the secluded chalet, Sloane discovers a hidden journal belonging to a man who once lived in Cabin 17—a place now rumored to be cursed. With her father's health deteriorating and her suspicions growing, Sloane enlists the help of her neighbor, a local handyman with his own troubled past, to investigate the cabin